ShadowSpinners

ShadowSpinners

A Collection of Dark Tales

Edited by Christina Lay

ShadowSpinners Press

.

Cover design by Pamela Herber

Cover art by MeCo

shadowspinnerspress.com

Table of Contents

INTRODUCTION   6

SWAMP SYMPHONY ◆ Cheryl Owen-Wilson   9

CHAIR ◆ Elizabeth Engstrom   15

THE MERCY OF MAGIC ◆ Christina Lay   23

CODEPENDENT SPECTRAL DISORDERS ◆ Eric M. Witchey   37

NO PATTERN BUT THE SEA ◆ Stephen T. Vessels   46

THE JINN MASTER ◆ Cynthia Ray   58

TRUE COLORS ◆ Pamela Jean Herber   70

FIVE TIPS FOR OUTSMARTING SATAN—AND YOUR STUDENTS   77
    ◆ Sarina Dorie

REDUCE. REUSE. RECYCLE. ◆ Alexis Duran   99

EILEEN AND THE ROCK ◆ Lisa Alber   108

THE PREMATURE WAKE OF MICHAEL MALONEY   127
    ◆ Alan M. Clark

A DARKQUICK SKY ◆ Matthew Lowes   152

Introduction

Welcome to *ShadowSpinners: A Collection of Dark Tales*. Congratulations on purchasing, borrowing or stealing this book. You are about to embark on a very interesting literary journey.

The tag line for the ShadowSpinners blog is "when nice people write bad things." The writers whose works are included in this collection are nice people, mostly, in the daylight. But get us alone with our characters and bad things tend to happen. We've all written stories that have scared the wits out of friends and have earned us the question, often asked with a nervous chuckle, "Where on earth do you get these ideas?"

That is indeed an excellent question. Several of us have addressed it on the blog, but while pondering how to introduce this rather eclectic collection, it came to me once again. Why do nice people write bad things? And what exactly makes a tale dark, anyway?

Within this volume you'll find a broad compendium of styles, ranging from humorous to thoughtful to outright horrific. Yet there is a common thread, a dark undertow that explores the mysterious depths of the human psyche. The description "dark" can mean so many things, but in this volume the sense of something obscured, veiled by shadow, underlies each story, whether we are hearing the whispers of ghosts over the phone line, pondering the weight of a hollow existence, saving young souls from Satan or battling terrifying alien forces in the void of space.

Often, the darkness, the ghost, resides in our own minds. And when faced with an outside force of evil, an equal and opposing force may arise from within. Whether our characters will meet evil with evil or with an overcoming, triumphant strength is the question at the heart of many of these stories.

If you're the sort of reader who likes to know what to expect, this might not be the volume for you. However, if you enjoy a rousing good yarn populated by fascinating characters in challenging situations, prepare to enjoy yourself.

Christina Lay
October 2015

Swamp Symphony

Cheryl Owen-Wilson

MY GRANDDADDY, HE THREW ME into the syrupy dark waters of the bayou when I was no higher than to his knees walkin' wobbly out to the end of the wharf he jus' built. Out on the island it was tradition, that when ya learnt to walk, ya learnt to swim. The rope wrapped 'round my waist cut through my threadbare cotton dress. I still got the scar on my hip where it rubbed down to the bone afore my daddy pulled me back in. The water tasted like dirt and grass and somethin' else, somethin' I have ever since tried to find.

That's my first memory, swamp water takin' my breath away and the smell of my daddy's beer-breath when he breathed it right back into me. I am the only Doucette who never learnt to swim. Maybe that's why, maybe if I'd a learnt to swim, maybe. I am my momma's only daughter and her very las' chil'. After birthin' eight afore me, her body had 'bout give up by the time I come out. But she lived, she lived to the age 102, she lived. And I lived right 'long with her. Well in a manner of speakin', I lived right 'long with her.

The camp, that's what my relations call my home; the camp, is smack dab in the middle of a boot-shaped island. The land is jus' enough to hold the camp and all the other buildings my daddy, Uncle Joe and granddaddy built. The only way off 'in the island is by pirogue. My Uncle Joe says you have to know the way or else you could get lost like my Uncle Ray did. He left one day and never found his way back, my grandmamma used to say sometimes she heard him cryin', sayin' he's tryin' to get home, but the bayou has too many fingers and he just can't find which one is pointin' homewards. Now my granddaddy, he used to say ain't no reason to ever leave, that we got everythin' we need right here. Squirrels, crawdads, gator and fish for eaten and our garden for greens. He said my grandmamma makes the best dandelion salad in all of Lafouche Parish.

The buildin's in the camp look like a snake, since they got added onto with each new baby or relation that come to live on the land. When they finally stopped comin' we had six bedrooms all tacked on and one room not attached, for cookin' further on out back. The outhouse is even further back; I 'member it was a mighty scary walk as a young chil'.

But my favorite place wasn't in one of those rooms, it was sleepin' on the porch when it got so hot you could cook an egg right on my momma's outside eatin' table. No really, you could; cause my brother John Jr. did one day, jus' to show me it would fry. Granddaddy had to take two pirogues all the way to St. Mary's Parish to get the metal screening for that porch, to keep the skeeters out. I would lay out in that porch on my feather mattress—feathers, I plucked my very own self out of those chickens that run free 'round the camp—and listen to what my granddaddy called, the swamp symphony. That's the sound all the critters make when the sun goes down. They do make quite a ruckus at certain times of the year. Since I never dared ask my granddaddy what a symphony was, I guess it's somethin' that sounds like a'lotta critters talkin' to one another. Yes the island was a grand place for a chil' to run from one end to the other, to live in trees, to always smell of mud and the things that crawl under the marshy ground. The island was great for a chil', but then I grew up to be a woman.

"Lizbeth, Lizbeth where are you?" I can hear her whispery voice callin' to me. I am sittin' on the stump of the last cypress tree my granddaddy ever cut down 'fore a gator cut him down. Sliced him right in two. His top half was layin' on the land and the other half was goin' down into the muddy waters with the gator. We was diggin' for crawdads when the gator got him. His top half was laughin' and tellin' me not to forget the bucket when his breathin' left him. I took the bucket up to my momma and told her. She yelled to my brother. "William Dean you go on down and give that gator the other half, it's wha' daddy would' a wanted." That's the last time my momma ever said anythin' 'bout her daddy. I don't think she liked him much, but I miss him sorely. It's like an ache in my stomach even after all these years he's been feedin' the gators down below.

I always come down here to get away from her when that ache gets real bad. Her and me we don't get on well. Been quite some time since we said kind words to the other, quite some time. Started when she fricasseed my pet squirrel Jimmy Joe. He was my only friend. I found him the night the island almost went under for good. The rain was comin' down so hard it left red marks on my skin for days after it stopped. I was runnin' to get to cover when I tripped right over the squirrel. I thought I squished the life from him cause when I got him in the house there was no air in him. But, then I saw his bushy gray tail move. He never left my room after that night. He stayed up on my bed with me while I watched the porch get eaten up by the waters and heard the wind rippin' up trees and throwin' em like they was nothin' but tiny bits of twig. That wind took my Daddy for his las' ride that night, I watched him pass right by my bedroom window like he was a flyin' bird. We found him a few days later, after the water let us leave the camp. He was layin', like he was nappin' peaceful as you please, in the top of one of the trees the wind left planted in the ground.

After we planted daddy—momma didn't want to feed him to the bayou—that's when the boys started leavin'. When Eddie Lee left, he was the last, he told momma he would send someone round to check on us from time to time. That someone was Johnny Dale. He give me my first store bought dress. He said Eddie Lee bought it in

N'Orleans. That was for my 14th year. That night after I put my dress on and did up my hair, Johnny Dale danced with me on the porch. That's what he called it, dancin'. I'd never danced afore; then he kissed me, real nice and slow like. Momma come out then and said supper was ready. I could smell the roux and onions when we walked to the table. Momma served us up each a big helpin'. She served us up Jimmy Joe Squirrel for our dinner, my birthday dinner. Didn't tell me till I had cleaned my plate dry. Ever time I smell roux cookin' now I think of Jimmy Joe Squirrel.

Johnny Dale, he come round more and more after that night and momma she got more and more mean spirited. One day I come in to find my store bought dress had become new curtains swayin' in momma's bedroom window. That's when I figured out what that taste was so long ago in my first memory; when I almost drowned. It was the taste of bein' free. Bein' free from the island, bein' free from the camp and finally bein' free from momma. My momma, who forever chained me with the guilt that without me there she would surely die, my momma, who said I would never survive offin' the island.

Johnny Dale and I planned it right here on this tree stump. He would come and get me, we would get married and live in a fine house with runnin' water right on Canal Street in N'Orleans. I waited. I waited all the nightlong and into the next night I waited. Johnny Dale never come and when I finally went back to the camp, there was my momma trompin' round in boots jus' like Johnny wore. Said he brought 'em to her the last time he come, swore on daddy's grave he brought 'em to her. Johnny Dale never come and neither did my bleedin' that month.

My momma, she pulled my beautiful dark-haired Rose Lyn out of me on the same feather mattress I was borned on. I never saw her, my baby, not with human eyes anyways. I never held her, not with human arms anyways. Momma, she took her away, singin' sweetly in her ear like she used to sing to me, she was singin' to Rose Lyn, when

I heard the paddle hit the water and in my mind's eye I could see the pirogue slidin' into the bayou. My body was slidin' too; it was slidin' away. I could feel the wet slidin' onto the mattress, then I smelt it, it smelt like holdin' an old rusty nail up to my nose, it felt like the whole bayou was flowin' from my body. It bled—it bled rose red— spreadin' out on the cotton tickin' like a flower openin' its petals. My breath left that body, jus' as my momma threw my baby girl over the side callin' to the gators that food was comin' and that she had to get back to me. She had to get me up so I could take care of her dinner. "That girl ain't got time for no baby, not when she got me to take care of." That's what my momma was sayin', as my baby girl lay at the bottom of the bayou on a bed of oozin' mud.

My first memory after my breath left, was now I can leave, now I am free. I could finally taste that taste from so long ago and it was bein' free. But the island, the camp, my momma, my Rose Lyn all had ahold of me like they was that rope wrapped round my waist pullin' me back down, back down into the muddy waters of the Atchafalaya swamp.

So here I sit, I can hear my momma callin' me. But she ain't here no more. She's long gone. Took me awhile. First I got rid of the pirogue so she was bound to the island. Then I took my time, showin' myself now and again. Showin' how I could take her food. Showin' how I could touch her skin with my cold hands. Showin' how many times her walkin' cane could go missin'. Showin' how brittle her bones were when she fell. Then I led her out to the stump and I showed her the bottom of the bayou. Nothin' kept her here when her time come. She went where she belonged, deep down under to be food for the gators, for all eternity, food for the gators.

My Rose Lyn, well I did get to hold her once and gaze down at her beautiful little face afore I had to give her over to the light waitin' cross the bayou for her innocent little soul.

And here I sit waitin', waitin'.

Moss sways in a gentle breeze, while night creatures make their rounds silently slithering over mud packed ground, then disappearing slowly into the bayous welcoming warmth. From the slap of the gators tail to the sudden croak of a bullfrog, it is a swamp symphony. Step to the edge of the island and peer into the blackness and you will see. It all began and ended with the wailing a tiny dark-haired girl, her piercing cries can still be heard on nights when the moon catches the light in that room, the room where she was born, the room where she entered the light for the first time and then embraced the dark.

"Y'all come for a visit soon please, the gators, they are a gettin' hung-gry."

The writing bug first snagged **Cheryl Owen-Wilson** through her penning of a personal essay, for which she received an award and publication. Today, short story fiction is what drives her writing, with an emphasis on Southern Gothic. Since her roots are buried deep in the bayous of Southern Louisiana, it is a natural fit. She is the mother of eight children, so family and all it entails is also prominent in her fiction. "Writing gothic tales featuring the dead is very natural to me, because in the south we live with our dead. They walk beside us and talk to us daily." When not visiting the mysteries of her childhood home she also writes fantasy and science fiction.

Chair

Elizabeth Engstrom

FOR SOME REASON, AS CLAIRE TRUDGED to work early on a Tuesday morning, instead of keeping her eyes straight ahead—or down on the cracked and pitched sidewalk to make sure she didn't trip—she looked left, down Second Street.

Second Street dead-ended at the Plant, and there, on the weedy lawn filled with dandelions, a man sat on a folding chair, his face held up to the early morning sun.

Scandalized, Claire pulled her sweater tight around her bony ribcage and hurried on to work. "Looney," she muttered.

The next day, Claire didn't need to look, and she knew she shouldn't have, but her eyes betrayed her as she hustled across Second Street, and she chanced a glance.

He was there, and this time there was a second chair, an *empty* chair, next to him.

This looked like an invitation, and Claire started to walk quickly toward her job in the zipper factory, where she had worked for decades, and knew everything about her job there was to know. She was comfortable in her little apartment, she was comfortable doing her job, and except for the days when the weather made it dangerous to walk the six blocks to work, her routine suited her.

But now this man and his apparent invitation bothered her, so much that she thought about him at work and wondered why he would sit so close to the Plant with its ominous blank gray concrete walls, and before she knew it, she cut a zipper one centimeter too short. The eye in the ceiling saw it immediately and dispatched a drone to escort her upstairs.

"Your mind is not on your work, Claire," the supervisor said.

Claire kept her eyes on the toes of her shoes. She didn't like looking at the supervisor. For one thing, his facial features were disproportionate in a very unattractive way, and he continually twirled a rubber band around his fingers which made her nervous, and for another thing, she didn't want him to think she was insubordinate.

"I'm sorry, sir," she said. "It won't happen again."

"It's not just one zipper, Claire," the supervisor said.

She wished he wouldn't say her name. She didn't want the sound of her name to come from his ugly mouth.

"We don't want it to become a trend. We don't want this to be the first of a whole series of accidents and mishaps, do we?"

"No, sir," Claire said.

"Is something bothering you? It's my job, you know, to help people who have troubles. We don't want people with troubles working here at Worldwide Zipper."

"No, sir, no troubles. I just lost my concentration for a moment."

"A moment is all it takes, Claire," he said, only this time he put some kind of a weird drawn-out accent on her name, to make it sound like he was mocking her. She feared she would hate her name from this moment on.

"It won't happen again."

"Back to work!" he commanded, and the door opened and the drone appeared at her side.

Chagrined, Claire returned to her work station and made certain she measured correctly for the rest of the day.

The next day, she woke up to a light rain, so she dressed warmly and carried her compact black umbrella, but once again, she could not keep her eyes to herself, and as she glanced over, the man was sitting next to the tall fence that surrounded the Plant, a huge colorful umbrella covering both him and the empty chair next to him.

He smiled at her. She could see his teeth, even two blocks away, a sure sign of lunacy. Heat flushed through Claire's face and she hurried on to her job, vowing to take a different route home and find a different way to work the next day that didn't provide such uncomfortable temptations as to look at the crazy man sitting in the weedy lot next to the razor wire fence.

But it wasn't the man who troubled her all day at work, it was the empty chair, the quiet, peaceful invitation to join him sitting there in the weeds, smiling, next to the wall of the Plant. What could he want with her? What could he be thinking and doing over there all by himself, with a chair that just anyone could come along and sit down in?

By the end of her workday, Claire had begun to worry that someone else would be sitting in that chair the next morning.

She got up early, hesitation in every action, but worry that someone else would be sitting in her chair gave her purpose. Filled with worry and anxiety, she left her apartment and strode toward Second Street.

He was there, sitting in the sunshine.

He waved at her.

She put her head down and walked toward him, down the unfamiliar sidewalk, across the street and didn't even hesitate when she stepped onto the grass of the weedy lot. She walked directly to the empty chair and sat down.

"Hi," the man said.

Claire didn't exactly feel the need to communicate with him, but she didn't want to be rude. "Hi," she answered.

They sat in silence for a good four minutes before she got up. She didn't want to leave his side, didn't want to leave the weeds, didn't want to leave the extraordinarily comfortable chair, even though it was just a little green folding chair, but to stay and lose her job was inconceivable, so she got up and hurried off to work.

The next day she got up earlier, and sat in his chair a couple of minutes longer.

The next day she got up even earlier, and sat in his chair even longer.

And the next day was her day of rest. She got up and got dressed as usual, and walked toward the weedy lot and the man in the chair.

He was there, as usual, and this time she had no reason to hurry away. A calming peace came over her as she sat next to him, just sitting quietly in the early morning sunshine.

"Companionship," he said. His voice had a melodic quality she had never heard before, and she had to consciously keep herself from looking at him in open-mouthed amazement. She wanted to stare at him, to drink in every detail of his face, but she dared not even look at him.

Companionship. She had heard that word before, but had never really understood the concept until this very moment. What a great idea. She loved companionship.

The sun rose high in the sky and still they sat, not talking. Claire began to think of her future, of possibilities she had never considered before. She wanted to take up a pencil and draw things. She wanted to draw his picture, and wondered if she even had a pencil or paper in her apartment. In a strange way, she couldn't quite remember what her apartment looked like, nor what she did at her job. Not while she was sitting next to this intriguing man, not while she was sitting in the shadow of the Plant.

"It's leaking," the man said, when Claire stood up to leave because she was getting cold in the shadow of the wall.

She looked at him for the first time, and his face was gloriously soft and genuine. He smiled with even, strong teeth and crinkles at the corners of his kind eyes. "Leaking?"

He nodded. "The Plant is leaking. My son discovered it."

"Your son?"

He nodded, smiled a sad smile, turned inward, and rocked back and forth a little bit.

Claire wrapped her sweater around herself and walked away through the wet weeds.

"Come back tomorrow," he called after her.

Even though she knew the word, suddenly the idea of tomorrow was a fresh concept. A new feeling grew in her chest, and she looked forward, maybe for the first time ever, to tomorrow.

The next day, the man stood up when she approached, and began talking even before she sat down in the chair. He spoke with some urgency, as if he had to tell her everything in the ten minutes she had before she had to leave for work.

"My son saw the carts in the night from his bedroom window. They come out of little doors on the other side of the Plant and they go to certain houses in the city. We thought the Plant was closed or deserted or something, but it isn't. He found out that the houses where the carts went to were houses with new babies, and where people were dying."

That seemed so incredibly odd to Claire that it didn't even seem possible. Was her companion just a lunatic after all?

"We think they deliver hope," he said.

"Hope?" Claire didn't even know what that was.

The man sighed. "It's all in here." He cocked his head toward the Plant. "It's all in here, and now it's leaking. That's why I sit here, because it feels so good. That's why *you're* here."

He *was* crazy! Claire got up and ran. She ran all the way to the zipper factory and arrived out of breath. Her coworkers stepped away from her as if she had something contagious. Nobody ever ran in the city. There was nothing to run to, nothing to run from.

But Claire had found something so confusing that she ran from it, and now, suddenly, she wanted to run back to it.

She didn't know what she thought, except that she needed to

keep her mind on her job and she needed to go back to the Plant wall and sit in the weeds with the man again tomorrow.

But the next morning, he wasn't there.

Claire went to the empty area where his chairs used to be; she could still see the marks on the ground where their feet had mashed the weeds into the soggy soil. She stood in the space where her chair—at least she had come to view it as her chair—had sat, and she waited for him.

She closed her eyes and let the sun warm her face. She felt the hope emanating from the concrete walls of the Plant behind her, and her mind opened to a million possibilities. She never had to go back to the zipper factory, never had to face the ugly supervisor again. She could leave the city. She could just sit here and wait for the man to come back, and then go to live with him and his son and they could have hope together. They could sit right here in the sun together every day, and bring another chair and another and another and invite people to join them and find this same kind of newness. She could live in a little tent, right here next to the Plant and soak up all that was emanating from it.

Life was full of possibilities, as long as she was here, as long as she was close to the razor-wire fence.

She never wanted to leave.

"Claire!" Startled, she looked up, and the supervisor stood in the middle of the street. "Come along, or you'll be late for work."

Claire looked down at her shoes so she wouldn't have to look at his face. She didn't want to go to work. She wanted to stand right here. She wanted to run back to her little apartment and get a chair—two chairs—and drag them right back here to this spot, so that when the man came back, he'd have a place to sit and companion.

"Claire?"

"It's leaking," she said, and in a burst of compassion for the ugly supervisor who made her life so gray, she invited him to join her.

"Come here and feel it."

"It's toxic waste," he said. "You'll go mad."

"No," she said, wondering how it could be that she was talking to her supervisor in this manner. "It's leaking hope."

"I'll report you if you get contaminated," he said. "I had to report the man who has been sitting here all that time."

"Why?" she asked. "Why would you do that?"

"Someone had to," the supervisor said. "Come along now."

Claire stood quietly for a long moment, considering her options, then one step at a time, she walked toward him through the wet weeds.

"You will have to sit all day with wet feet," he said.

"Yes," she said, and then remembered.

"Didn't your wife just have a baby?" she asked.

"Yes. Two weeks ago."

So he had hope. He got a glass of it, or a package of it, or a dose of it, or something, just recently. He had it at home; he didn't have to sit in the weeds next to the concrete wall and the razor wire fence in order to feel it.

"How did the hope get inside the Plant?" she asked him as they walked toward the factory.

"The Plant is abandoned," he said. "There's nothing inside the building."

Claire didn't believe him, but the further she got from it, the less it mattered.

"What happens when you report someone?" she asked.

The supervisor opened the employee door to the Worldwide Zipper Factory. "That's not our concern," he said. "We're here to make zippers and make them correctly." He paused and looked at her. "I hope you don't go back there again. Nothing good will come of it."

There it was again, that word, hope.

She didn't answer him, but went straight to her work station and cut zippers to their perfect length all day long, and when she went home, she looked at the only chair in her apartment and thought about how it would look next to the fence, next to the Plant.

Pathetic, she decided. She had no second chair, she had no colorful umbrella. She could not companion.

In the morning, she left at the usual time for work. As she crossed Second Street, she glanced down, but nothing was there but the weedy lot, the razor wire fence and the gray wall of the Plant.

The supervisor was probably right, she thought. Toxic waste. Nothing good could come of it.

Elizabeth Engstrom is the author of fourteen books. Her latest novel is Baggage Check, a thriller, and her latest nonfiction is How to Write a Sizzling Sex Scene. She has a BA in Literature/Creative Writing, and an MA in Applied Theology, both from Marylhurst University. Her book Candyland was recently made into a major motion picture (Candiland). She lives in the Pacific Northwest with her fisherman-husband and their dog, where she is on the board of directors for Wordcrafters in Eugene (www.wordcraftersineugene.org). She teaches the occasional writing class, puts her pen to use for social justice, and is always working on her next book. www.ElizabethEngstrom.com

The Mercy of Magic

Christina Lay

VTALY HAD WALKED A LONG WAY on one good foot, and he was very tired. To be truthful, he had a foot and half, but the half-foot felt like no foot. It hindered instead of helped. Each time his resolve wavered and he was tempted to turn around and climb back up the well-worn steps to the castle, he found the motion too painful. So down he went, against his better judgment, against common sense, descending the steep staircase in limps and lurches.

The stairs clung to the hillside, plunging steeply towards the river. A parapet of crumbling brick lined the side of the path that overlooked the town, and he used it for support, breathing hard, both wishing and fearing someone might come along who could help him, but there was no one. Though night waned, dust and smoke thickened the darkness and obscured any lights from below. Spires and towers poked up here and there like lone ships on a black sea.

Blood loss and exhaustion had weakened him, and his mutilated foot hurt so badly it made him sick. He stopped to vomit. A bright mix of brandy and stomach bile splattered across his one shiny boot. As he wiped his chin with the cuff of his coat, he heard someone approaching.

A withered hand appeared on the low wall, and then an old vendor emerged from around the next twist in the staircase, where he paused to catch his breath. He held a tall pole. Dozens of silk scarves hung from the pole like remnants of a king's standard. Vtaly was very glad to see the man and his wares. He limped down to him and handed him a silver coin for a handful of scarves.

With a groan he sank onto a step and pulled off the blood-soaked linen napkin he'd wrapped around the stump of his left foot. The old man pocketed the coin and leaned on his pole, inspecting Vtaly with interest.

"Did you save the rest of it?" he asked, after a moment's consideration.

"What?" Vtaly glared up at him, having no desire to discuss the details of his misfortune with a stranger.

"Did you keep the toes?" the man asked, black eyes glittering.

"What of it?" Vtaly asked, reddening at the memory of scrabbling beneath the contessa's long dining room table, searching for his foot. He should have let it go. He could see that now. He should have stood his ground, half a foot or no. He should have laughed.

"Well, if you've got the rest of the foot, there's a woman who can fix it for you."

Vtaly looked up from the bloody mess in his hands.

"She can sew the foot back together?" he asked, doubtful, but keenly aware that he'd left the world of logic behind when he'd stepped his half foot on the staircase to old town. And wasn't magical intervention what he'd secretly hoped for all along?

"Mmmmm, not exactly. She finds a new bit, takes the old in payment."

"How wretched," Vtaly said, intrigued in spite of his revulsion. What did he have to lose, other than a lump of dead flesh?

"Her name is Mina. You'll find her in the commissary near the black tower."

"Thank you," Vtaly said. The old man had very black eyes and very grey skin. It was hard to tell if he had hair, or if the hissing gaslight and moonspun shadows merely painted make-believe strands on his shining skull. He sighed, thinking he might as well get used to such illusions if he planned to travel all the way to old town and search for this repellent healer. He already knew he would. He needed toes to climb back into the society from which he'd fallen, and he needed desperately to be whole. That's where he belonged. Not down here. The castle complex loomed far above him at the top of the hill, but that physical distance was no obstacle compared to his imperfection.

Having rewrapped his injured foot in colorful silk, he pushed up painfully on the whole one and took his leave of the overly curious vendor. More townsfolk climbed the stairs now, the sun rising despite his troubles. Other vendors took their places in archways and children ran up and down ferrying baskets of fish, bread and vegetables. No one paid any attention to the pale, limping man in the stylish velvet frock coat. As the sun broke free of the eastern hills, he stepped off the staircase onto the sloping street that led to the river and the stinking town that encrusted its banks.

Downward still, he noted, as the street opened onto a square. The buildings stood in varying states of decay, mere husks of their counterparts above. The cobblestoned area emitted an odor strong enough to penetrate his sweat-soaked musk. Goats filled the spaces not taken by unwashed bodies, carts, rickety stalls and rubble.

He leaned against a lamp pole, which still hissed in the dim light of dawn. A thick, sticky layer of dirt swirled and coated every surface. This was the bottom of earth's barrel, so close to the muddy crust it had become mud, people and all. In the untrustworthy light, they all looked like ghosts, and could well be, as far as Vtaly knew. But they smelled real enough.

How unlike that fantastic world from which he'd just descended! The contessa's court sparkled and glittered in eternal candlelight, gilt-edged and lavender-scented, its memory danced in his mind like a fading dream.

He looked up, to try to recapture the dream, and but could not see the castle or the cathedral. He shuddered and moved on. One must not linger too long, or the funk of the old town might become impossible to remove.

The black tower was easy enough to find, being entirely blackened with age and soot, and the tallest structure on the river, where it guarded the bridge. What had been an old guards' barrack stood beside it, and apparently the inhabitants of this realm used it as a gathering place, with many cook pots boiling and fires blazing in various corners and crannies. Long wooden tables filled the high-ceilinged room. Goats were there too, as well as chickens, pigeons, cats, dogs, and one small donkey. Slouched and dank people shuffled around him as he lingered in the doorway. They spoke the king's tongue but in thick accents that sounded foreign.

So this was old town. Vtaly wanted nothing to do with it. He grabbed at one ragged figure and shouted over the din,

"Where is Mina, the healer?"

The person, who turned out to be a small man, looked at him wide-eyed in surprise, shook his head, and scuttled away. Vtaly scowled, wondering how he'd ever find her in the chaos. When he stood up straight, which made his head spin, he was about a head taller than anyone else in the room. He felt many eyes upon him, but as he squinted into the gloom, the stares darted away. Only one did not.

The narrowed eyes of a woman, the only person sitting alone in the crowded room, lingered on his face just long enough for him to notice her. Then she returned her attention to her plate. She had a whole table to herself, and used it. Elbows out, arms thick and heavy, half empty bowls spread all around her, she hunkered over her meal like a wolf over a carcass. Vtaly had the sick feeling that this was the healer.

He hobbled over and collapsed onto the bench across from her. She glanced up briefly. Seaweed green eyes flickered over his expensive clothing with nary a reaction. She returned to her gristle, gnawing and slurping with big teeth and wide fleshly lips.

"Are you the healer?" he asked.

She kept eating, not looking at him, until the bone she held was stripped of flesh. She tossed it aside, wiped her lips with the back of her hand, and took a noisy swallow from a jar filled with thick creamy liquid. Vtaly tasted the bile rise in his throat, and fought down another bout of sickness.

"Can you afford it?" she asked, finally looking straight at him.

"I have crowns," he said. She snorted, some of her drink bubbling out of her nostrils.

"I have half a foot," he added.

She nodded. "Let's see it."

"What? Here? It's half a foot, ball and toes. What difference can it possibly—?"

"I'll see it or have none of you," she said. Vtaly grumbled a curse and reached into his pocket. He couldn't dally with the woman much longer. He felt unwell, and feared he might expire in this festering dump of a swill hall.

He placed the bloody bundle on the platter nearest him.

"Nice napkin," she said, fondling its corner with her stubby fingers. Surely when the stewards had set the contessa's table the evening before, they'd never imagined where that delicate piece of linen would end up.

She unwrapped the foot. He glanced around. No one paid any attention to their gruesome dealings. She harrumphed and poked at it with a fork.

"Fresh," she said.

"Quite," he snapped, suddenly agitated beyond endurance. "Can you help me or not?"

"I can. After I finish my meal." With the same fork, she dug into a pile of slop on her plate. All the plates started to spin and Vtaly's forehead hit the table with a soft thud. He suspected he retched again, but didn't care. Dimly aware of hands pulling at him, he regained awareness outside, in the cooler but still foul air of a black alley.

As his head cleared, he was surprised to find himself walking beside the woman, along remarkably uneven and upturned cobblestones. Her heavy hands clung to his arm. Tall and dilapidated houses cast the street in gloom, transforming the morning into a strange sort of twilight. They stopped before a daub and wattle house near the river. It had a tilted, melting appearance that made it look as if it had survived several floods. He seemed to remember hearing something of floods, but such things had never concerned him. He smelled the river, eons of it seeping from the stones.

As she wrestled a large key out of her cloak and jabbed it into a small wooden door, he looked up and over his shoulder. By chance the narrow street opened to a view of the castle. The mists parted, allowing its glassed windows to catch the remote sunlight. They flashed like stars high above the peaked roofs around them.

The door creaked open. The woman entered, swallowed by foul blackness. Vtaly hesitated, but where else could he go? He grabbed the doorframe, and stepped into a damp little room lit only by the smoldering remains of a hearth fire.

A match flared, and she lit a candle. The room contained two doubtful chairs, a large wooden table, an iron stove, and stacks upon stacks of crates, boxes, and sacks. A narrow staircase in the corner led to a second story. The place stank of wet dog, though he saw no evidence of one.

"Sit," she commanded, and Vtaly was happy to do so.

"How long will this take?" he asked.

"Days," she replied. He almost complained, but then remembered that a few hours ago, before he needed it, he wouldn't have believed such an operation was even possible, so he held his tongue.

"I must find a match for your foot," she said. She took the stump out again, and turned it this way and that in the dim light.

"What ever will you do with it?" he asked, curiosity getting the better of him. She glared at him without answering before walking to the steps. The whole house shuddered and groaned as she climbed. Even she could climb, he thought bitterly. But she couldn't climb to the castle. None of these people could. Vtaly could. He knew it and he must maintain that knowledge like a flame in his heart, or he would become stuck down here in the mud. He was sure of it. Panic clawed at him, and he wanted to yell after her to hurry up, but knew instinctively it wouldn't help. He picked up an iron poker and prodded the fire back to life, watching his future smolder and spark around the edges.

After a thousand nightmares entered and left his mind, and the candle burned down an inch, the woman returned to stand beside him, a small black box in her hand.

"You're pretty when you sleep," she said. "The smugness leaves you."

He sat up straight and wondered why he wasn't dead yet.

"I found the perfect thing," she said, and dragged the other chair near him.

"Thing?" he repeated, and realized he hadn't thought about that, about what she would use to fix his foot. He only wanted it done, and had little interest in the how. That was the stuff of myth, legend, hex and harrow. His rational mind had excused itself from further involvement, and so there he sat, at the mercy of magic.

Close up, the woman smelled of stale beer. Her skin was nearly translucent, like the sea creatures in the contessa's scientific menagerie. Her greasy hair was yellowish. She breathed meaty breath on him in her excitement.

"You're very lucky. Usually I'd have to go scavenging." She took the lid off the box and pulled out a small, scabby bird's foot, maybe two inches long.

Vtaly laughed. "You're joking."

"This is a jackdaw's foot," she said, scowling. "It's more than you deserve."

"Perhaps you should take your time, and come up with something more appropriate, like a horse's hoof or a tiger's paw."

"It doesn't work like that!" she shrieked. "The piece picks you, not the other way around."

"I merely meant—"

"Be still. I like you better when you sleep." She growled and stroked her bird foot as if it were a pet.

"It's too small."

"It will grow, idiot!" She pulled an empty crate close to them and patted it. "Put your half foot up here," she said. Vtaly did as ordered, though he felt himself falling deeper and deeper into unreality. Surely he'd wake up and realize he'd merely been drunk...that it had all been a terrible nightmare.

She unwrapped his foot, pocketing the bloody scarves. He braced himself for terrible pain, but apparently, the foot had gone numb. She massaged the stump, bending and twisting it, and he felt nothing. Nothing except her hot and surprisingly gentle fingers brushing his skin. She hummed and he drifted again, nearly asleep when the red-hot poker touched his raw wound.

This time when he regained consciousness, he lay on the floor in front of the fire, a rough wool blanket thrown over him and a grain sack beneath his head.

She means well, he thought, and instantly doubted it.

What did she do with the toes?

He sighed and noticed watery sunlight pooling on the warped floorboards beside him. Was it dusk or dawn? In the castle, would they be readying themselves for the nightly festivities or a morning excursion? He heard the cathedral bells ring, and imagined the smell of hot tea and sweet rolls in the sunroom. Sensed the hush of silk and satin on flawless skin, drifting along bright corridors.

Down here, the fire was dead. The woman was gone. He could tell by the quiet.

With a start, he remembered the jackdaw foot and sat up. He ripped aside the blanket and stared down. Grafted to his foot with rough stitches, three small, scrawny bird toes stuck out. It looked so ridiculous he had to laugh. He laughed until he cried.

Wiping away the tears, he wiggled his toes. They moved, just like his old ones did. Only these moved more. They curled and he imagined he could pick up twigs with them and dig for worms, like the jackdaws in the courtyard did. This caused a fresh round of hysteria. He supposed he must resign himself to always having sex with his boots on. What would the contessa think?

His amusement evaporated. Would he be allowed, in this state, to reenter the castle complex? Would he forever limp? Would they know how far he'd fallen?

At that moment, the woman burst through the front door.

"Oh, you're awake," she said.

She looked less disgusting in the brighter light, perhaps a bit less greasy without shadows sliding off her.

"I'll go now," he said.

"Don't be an idiot!" she shouted, then more calmly said, "It has to have a chance to take root, to grow."

"I can move them," he said, and demonstrated.

"Of course you can! You think I do shoddy work? What good are toes you can't move?" She grumbled and crouched before the hearth, tossing in dried twigs and leaves. He climbed to his knees and pulled up onto a chair, reluctant to put weight on his new foot.

"How long?" he asked.

"Days," she said again. They stared at each other. She looked away first.

"Do you want to see?" she asked.

"See what?"

"What's become of your old foot."

"No," he said. "Do you have any tea? I'll pay."

She snarled and called him an idiot. She made the tea, foul, bitter stuff. As they drank out of metal tankards she asked him again about viewing his old foot, glancing at him slyly like an excited child.

He decided he'd better humor her, if he were to recuperate there on her floor for another day or two.

"Come," she said, and headed up the stairs.

"I don't think I can."

"Don't be a baby. Of course you can."

He nervously stood, shuffling without putting weight on the new toes. He stood at the bottom of the steep stairs until she reached the top. He sighed and took a step up. The new toes curled efficiently around the drooping lip of each step, and he was able to hop lightly the whole way up. He felt quite hopeful by the time he reached the landing, sure now that he could return to the castle that very day. His elation vanished at the sight that awaited him.

"This is Damek," she said proudly. "Your foot fit him perfectly."

On the bed sat a man-thing. A patched together creature of mannish shape, with two legs, two arms, a body and head, but all mismatched. There indeed were his toes, attached to a man's heel, ankle and shin, but some sort of horse thigh. The other leg looked doglike, maybe a wolf, being so large. The skin, or hide, was part fur, part scales, part flesh. Bits of fabric hung here and there forming some semblance of clothing. Vtaly's vision blurred, and he feared he might swoon again, but he couldn't stop staring.

The man thing had mismatched eyes, one human, one cat. He had a small beak for a nose and human lips. The left arm was a vulture's wing with a large cat's paw attached, the other something akin to an orangutan. Vtaly thought the woman must be plundering the cast-off remains of the castle's zoological park. It was too much to take in, and he turned away, leaning a hand against the wall.

"Why would you make such a creature?" he asked.

To his surprise, she laughed. "Ah, fallen man, you of all people would ask me that?"

He peeked over his shoulder. She stroked its head and it smiled, apparently not at all disturbed by this fate.

"You, fallen man, I sew you back together, better than before, and then you leave. They all leave. Damek won't leave me alone."

"No, I don't suppose he will." Vtaly calmed his breathing. He had to remember where he was, old town. Mud town. Nothing was real here. They did not reason as modern man had learned to, nor believe in science, nor separate dream from day. He must leave today. Now.

"I'll go now," he said.

"Your toes aren't ready."

"They work fine. Thank you."

In a perfectly cultured voice, Damek asked, "Where are you going?"

Vtaly nearly fell down the stairs in shock. He'd expected grunts and growls.

"To the castle," he said.

"It's very pleasant there. I'll help you."

"What? You've never been there!" Every superior fiber of Vtaly's being rebelled against this claim.

"He has," Mina said, smiling. "Not so long ago."

"That's impossible! He can't exist there!" Vtaly's head spun, and he started down the stairs. Down was harder, and he flapped his left elbow to keep his balance, hindered by the walls that leaned in around him.

Damek came behind him, followed by Mina.

"You will help each other!" she called after them.

Vtaly stopped in the doorway. "You may not come with me," he said firmly. The creature was taller than him, and steadier on his new foot.

"You won't make it without help. It's too far and you are not finished."

Vtaly stared into the two mismatched eyes with difficulty. He detected no malice there, only childlike glee at the thought of going on an excursion. Perhaps the thing could help him up the stairs, and then he could lose him, either as he burned up in the light of the pure sun, or when the castle guards prevented him from going further, as they surely must.

Vtaly nodded curtly, then threw the rest of his coins on the floor for Mina.

This is the worst yet, he thought, as he hurried down the street, followed closely by the man-thing. Down here in the mud, no one looked twice at the strange duo, and he found himself laughing. He noticed bright buttons on the ragged velvet jacket that hung over Damek's ape shoulder, and then he spied the castle shining above them, a jewel, a morsel of light. He lusted after it, and walked with a spring in his new foot, his vision warped by jackdaw thoughts.

The stairs did present a challenge for him, and he found himself wishing for a wing like Damek had, then shoved this thought roughly aside. He allowed the creature to assist him, grabbing his ape arm and leaning on him for support. He decided to guide him to the cathedral, which would be empty. He held on to the hope that the nightmare beside him could not survive the highest and brightest spot in the land.

When they reached the top of the hill, the slanted sunlight pierced his eyes, and he finally knew it was evening. He rushed across the open square to the massive church. Again, no one took notice and he dared not question why. Damek strode easily beside him, taking in the wonders of fresh air and light with a smile on his horrible face.

Vtaly stood before the massive doors of the church.

"Go home now, Damek," he said, but Damek did not go, so with a shrug, Vtaly pushed open the doors and walked in. The rays of the sun cascaded in through the massive stained glass windows, painting the walls in sapphire, emerald and vermillion strokes.

Damek strode without hesitation into the sanctuary, and still he did not vanish. This weighed heavily on Vtaly's heart. Even the pure, clean lines of the soaring arches could not cheer him. The man-thing seemed happy, meandering up the aisle along the empty pews, humming an ancient hymn.

"Mina is waiting for you," Vtaly called across the echoing space, without much hope. It wasn't actually his problem, he decided, unless the creature continued to follow him. He would leave him there and return to the court, demonstrating to all how he harbored no ill will nor suffered any ill effects from his injury. With luck, no one would even remember what had caused his sudden absence. Unpleasant things were not allowed in the castle.

Just before he turned to sneak out, the creature knelt down before the altar, bowed his head, and pressed his palms together. It took a moment for Vtaly to recognize this as prayer, and he thought how odd it seemed to see someone praying in the church, which had been a temple to man's accomplishments for much longer than it had ever been the seat of a bishop.

It dawned on him that the creature, being from old town, believed in God. He shook his head and left the illusion to his delusion. He walked out into the brilliant sunlight, his three toes clicking and clacking against the cobblestones. He would need to get a new boot, to hide his imperfection. He headed for the castle, but oddly enough, found himself on the stairs again, going down.

When he reached Mina's house, he knelt before where she sat, and rested his head against her wide breasts.

She patted his shoulder.

"Perhaps you'd like me to replace the other foot," she said, extracting a rat's paw from her pocket.

A native of Eugene, Oregon, **Christina Lay** attended the University of Oregon in Eugene and now works there in a Victorian House Museum keeping an eye out for ghosts. She's completed four novels and started so very many more. Her fiction has won several awards, including first place in the Rupert Hughes Prose Writing Competition at the 2000 Maui Writer's Conference. Her novel *Death is a Star*, a contemporary fantasy, was published by IFD Publishing in 2013. She's had several short stories appear in anthologies spanning several genres. She enjoys writing, reading about writing, attending writers' conferences and workshops, and talking endlessly about writing with her dog and four and a half cats. You can find her non-fiction work at christinalay.wordpress.com and shadowspinners.wordpress.com.

Codependent Spectral Disorders

Eric M. Witchey

THE FIREMEN WERE COMING. THAT'S ALL I'D GOTTEN from my son. My heart grew colder under layers of sonic snow, each layer made of another second of hissing silence on my cell. Pinching the phone between my shoulder and ear, I plucked another HO model train wheel-and-axle set from the loose pile on my vinyl work mat. The snow storm hiss assaulted my ear while I examined the wheels and set them into the plastic sorting tray compartment I had hand lettered, "HO. Wheel. RP25. Freight. 33 scale inches. Metal. Flat black. Blunt axle pin." While my hands moved, my mind worked the puzzle of talking to my son.

"Use his full name, our family therapist, 'Cassandra Victoria Fanterri, Ph.D. Please, Call me Cassie,'" had said.

"His name can cut through the fog of his sensory overload," Cassie *had said.*

"Be firm, not angry. That means level tone and relaxed facial muscles."

Except, I didn't need to worry about the face thing because I was on the phone.

I picked up another set of wheels and took a deep breath. "Randall Phillip Crawly. Was anyone hurt?"

I hoped my stern use of his full name would shift his focus—jump whatever mental train he had going onto a new track.

I needed him on my track. I didn't have time for his spectrum problems. Not now. Once emergency services arrived, Randy would overload like an antique Rivarossi headlight on DCC rails. He'd get bright for a second, then he'd go dark.

I located the wheels' compartment in the tray—*HO Wheel. RP25. Freight. 33 scale inches. Metal. Flat black. Pointed axle pin.* I had a Bettendorf truck frame it would fit.

If he would just tell me what had happened, I'd know what to do next. If he would give his mother the phone—

I picked up another wheel set.

HO. Wheel. RP25. Freight. 33 scale inches. Silver. Pointed axle pin.

I wanted to scream a dozen questions into my cell. I wanted to know about Alma, Randy's mother, but I held my tongue. Before Cassi had insulted Alma and given up on us, she had taught me that if my son were going to come around to what I needed, I had to wait. Speaking again would only give him an excuse to retreat, to get back on his track and lose any progress that following the therapist's suggestion had given me.

Somewhere, wires crossed or microwaves tangled. Faint voices held ghostly conversations just beyond my ability to understand. I sorted wheels and waited for my son to answer.

A woman laughed. Even ghosts laugh. In her distant voice, I heard flirt and hope. Guiltily, I wished she were my wife—that I was talking to her. Alma's voice had lost that tone long ago.

Waiting for Randy to speak was a war. The winner would be the one who held his tongue longest.

My neck cramped. I shifted the phone to my other ear and held it with my shoulder.

HO. Wheel. RP25. Freight. 33 scale inches. Brass. Pointed axle pin.

If Alma were hurt, every second mattered, but any words I uttered could add countless minutes to the phone call. I didn't dare heap disaster on disaster. I couldn't, not any more than I could drop my "HO. Wheel. RP25. Freight. 33 scale inches. Black plastic. Pointed axle pin." into the tray for "HO. Wheel. RP25. Freight. 33 scale inches. Metal. Flat black. Pointed axle pin."

If I did make things worse and she died, who would raise Randy?

The waiting and the ghosts had almost beaten me down. I nearly dropped a 36 scale inches wheel in a 33 scale inches compartment. I was drawing breath to try and break Randy's silence again when I smelled oil. While I scanned my workbench for an open, pinky-sized squeeze tube of light, non-conductive axle oil, Randy spoke.

"She was telling me about the ferret she had when she was a kid his name was Loki and he was a rescue from the pet shop in the strip mall down the street nobody wanted him because he was crazy and his name means crazy like a tricky god from the Norse Pole."

New track. Wrong track. I had won the wrong war.

The ghost woman giggled. For just a moment, I understood her words. "I like that," she said.

I couldn't find the open oil. It should be easy. I always put it in the brass pen tray in the upper right quadrant of my workbench. Always! Even if I'd forgotten, the tube was striped like a barber pole in caution orange and fluorescent green. I should have been able to see it instantly.

"RANDALL!" It just burst out of me. I couldn't stop it, and I couldn't get it back.

Cold, cell-snow silence filled my ear. I decided I regretted my blurt.

I found the tube of oil, capped it, and dropped it in the pen tray.

I knew my son's atypical brain as well as anyone, except maybe Alma, and while my freezing heart pushed out another slow motion surge of blood, my burning imagination created horrible variations on disaster for Alma.

The Cassie-trained part of me chanted the mantra, *sympathy for poor Randy.* He couldn't help it. For just an instant, my imagined Alma-empty kitchen and silent vacuum cleaner gave way to an image of my son, his high forehead wrinkled in concentration, his eyes watering, his shoulders rolled forward like he was pushing his way into a blizzard to get the mail through to some remote town in the outback of some story world where Alma would reward his heroics with kind words, a warm hearth, and respect.

But it was Randy, and we don't live in a story world. Randy is what he is.

OO. Wheel. Hornby. Freight. Special 40 scale inches. Brass. Prewar clip mount axle.

The silence was not as long this time.

He began his story again. When derailed, he always had to begin again. He never picked up where he left off like norm—like typical people. "She was telling me about the ferret she had…."

I swallowed hard, wondering why my mouth wasn't dry like it was supposed to be, like all the people in the stories mouths were when they were scared. Instead of the emotions Cassie said were normal, anger, fear, and frustration, turning my mouth dry or transforming the spit in my mouth to caustic bile, my mouth felt normal. In fact, once I started thinking about it, it felt better than it usually did—warm, wet, and ready to kiss poor Alma if she had been at home taking care of me like she promised instead of running Randy to the lessons she insisted he have.

The ghost woman spoke in a high, affected, dramatic voice. "I don't *think* so!"

HO. Wheel. RP25. Freight. 33 scale inches. Metal. Flat black. Pointed axle pin.

Ignoring the distant whispering and the cell's electronic hiss, I wondered how my mind could fill the cold silence with thoughts about how my mouth should be? It was a horrible, simple thought, and I wished terrible guilt would chase it away. I wanted to feel different, to feel how I should feel in a moment when lives are changing forever.

HO. Wheel. RP25. Freight. 33 scale inches. Metal. Flat black. Pointed axle pin.

Later, if something really bad had happened, those thoughts about my mouth and the flirting ghost would become recycled regrets intruding on quiet moments every day for the rest of my life. They would intrude unannounced and unwanted the same way Randy's name had leapt from my mouth at the worst possible moment.

Randy started again.

I forced myself to focus—forced myself to listen as if listening more carefully would provide more meaning than his repeated words carried.

"…Norse Pole they took it home and built it a giant cage that you could walk into so you could play with the ferret without it getting—"

HO. Wheel. RP25. Freight. 33 scale inches. Metal. Flat black. Pointed axle pin.

"—out and making things crazy in the house like its name but in a cage instead of everywhere."

Sometimes, I could finish pieces of the story Randy needed to tell. Sometimes, if I saw ahead a little ways and gave his brain a bridge from the now of the tale in his head to a new now, his brain would let him cross that bridge.

Sometimes.

I tried. "And they loved Loki, and Mom was driving while she told you the story. It was raining hard."

"Yeah. Uh-huh."

The ghost woman's background drone solidified. "Terrible weather, but I like that…." It trailed off into the background hiss.

Such a sweet voice, but she was talking to someone else. I should have bit my lip. I should have held my breath. I should have felt tears on my cheeks. I should have felt something instead of worrying about what I didn't feel and how it would bother me later.

HO. Wheel. RP25. Freight. 33 scale inches. Brass. Blunt axle pin.

I shouldn't have been thinking about what the ghost lady said or my breath or my lip. I knew what I shouldn't think, but I didn't know what I should think so I could look back on the moment with less guilt for all my non-Alma thoughts.

I decided to put the phone on speaker and prop it against a locomotive on the workbench, an Athearn AMD F3 in Great Northern livery. Then, I stretched my shoulder before I remembered to bite my lip. The bite hurt, but that's all. It didn't cause me to feel what I should have felt.

Randy said, "…and raining and the windshield wipers were going really fast but it was still raining so hard it was hard to see she asked me about school she said, 'How's school going, Randy?' and I said, 'Okay.' and she said, 'I'm glad. You know you can ask me for help anytime.'"

How could I not love a woman who demanded piano lessons for your spectrum disorder son then drove him to them and back during a tornado-spawning thunder-banger? How could I not feel love for a woman who, even in the storm, was still patient enough to offer Randy kindness that might move him out of his normal, deeply rutted patterns? How could anybody not feel love for a woman like that?

Cassie and her labels. If Alma was hurt, it was Cassie's fault.

HO. Wheel. Flat Flange. Freight. 33 scale inches. Metal. Flat black. Pointed axle pin.

The hissing phone crackled. Ghostly words came to my ear. "Love." Then, all the false coquettishness gone from her voice, the ghost laughed deep and hard. While her laughter faded into the static blizzard, I thought of Alma's hip next to mine the time we were car-trapped on a secondary road near the summit of the Sherman grade on the Union Pacific in a Wyoming blizzard.

Our first time happened that night—my first, ever. I was so

grateful. I still don't know what she saw in me. I was almost thirty. No other woman had seen what she saw.

The trooper found us naked in the back seat, our parkas, blue jeans, and sweatshirts folded and stacked on the front seat. Standing in the storm peering in through the gapped window, he laughed at me.

I felt rage. I felt *that*. I started to yell at him.

Alma gripped my arm, nails cutting into my red rage. In my ear, she said, "I know how to take care of you. I will always take care of you."

It didn't make sense, but it grabbed my thoughts and made me look at her. Her dark eyes sparkled in the beam of the trooper's Mag Light. She smiled, looked him in the eye, and said, "We're warmer than you are." He stopped laughing. Still smiling, he said, "I guess you are."

HO. Wheel. RP25. Freight. 33 scale inches. Metal. Flat black. Pointed axle pin.

Randy kept talking. I missed some of his tale. He said, "She said, 'You know your Dad loves you,' and she said she did too."

"I'm almost out of minutes," the ghost said.

Randy went quiet. The phone hissed.

I wondered if he could hear the ghostly woman.

I could hear him breathing faster. He had to say something he didn't want to say. "She said, 'He's hard, you know—your Dad.'"

I know she had said it tone and syllable-for-sad-syllable exactly as he had. Randy's mind couldn't let him say it any other way.

HO. Wheel. RP25. Freight. 33 scale inches. Metal. Flat black. Pointed axle pin.

HO. Wheel. RP25. Freight. 33 scale inches. Silver. Blunt axle pin.

"'He's a little like you, Randy. He's hard. You have to know when to listen and when to talk.'"

In sessions, Cassie had said it to me over and over. "Listening is more than being quiet."

Now, I had to listen. I had to listen if I ever wanted a bowl of Alma's chowder on a cold winter day, if I ever wanted her hip next to mine, if I ever—

"'but you can't expect him to hear you, you know Randy? You have to know that.'"

Silence. Not even the ghost lady spoke. New layers of cell phone snow became heavier and heavier until I thought my heart would just stop.

"She said, 'There's a train coming, Randy.' And I said an EMD SD 70 Mac and she said, 'You can tell from the sound?' and I said yeah."

A distant siren broke through the phone's filters for a second. Emergency vehicles were arriving. Noise. Flashing lights. I knew that soon Randy wouldn't be able to say anything, tell me anything.

HO. Wheel. RP25. Freight. 33 scale inches. Metal. Flat black. Pointed axle pin.

"People." Randy spoke the word like most people would say "spider" or "snake." He knew he was about to be hit by a wave that would drown out all his own thoughts. "People, Dad." It was a plea for help.

"They are going to help." I tried to sound confident.

"It was really rainy really really rainy she stopped telling me stuff she stopped the car she just stopped no Loki no piano. She said, 'No more enabling, Randy.' She made me get out in the rain she said, 'Your Dad loves his trains.'"

HO. Wheel. RP25. Freight. 33 scale inches. Metal. Flat black. Pointed axle pin.

HO. Wheel. RP25. Freight. 33 scale inches. Metal. Flat black. Pointed axle pin.

HO. Wheel. RP25. Freight. 33 scale inches. Metal. Flat black. Pointed axle pin.

"She drove BANG I'm cold it's wet and rainy."

"Where's Mom, Randy?" I asked.

"People."

"Where is she?"

"Dad?"

"I'm here."

"She was in the car."

"Now. Where is she now?"

"Listen. Listen, Dad. Can't you hear her? Listen."

The phone snow stopped. I held my breath, my hands in my lap, waiting for the ghost to speak.

Eric Witchey has sold more than 100 stories. His stories have appeared in nine genres and on five continents. He has received awards or recognition from New Century Writers, Writers of the Future, Writer's Digest, The Eric Hoffer Prose Award Program, Short Story America, the Irish Aeon Awards, and other organizations. His How-to articles have appeared in The Writer Magazine, Writer's Digest Magazine, and other print and online magazines. When not teaching or writing, he spends his time fly fishing or restoring antique model locomotives.

No Pattern but the Sea

Stephen T. Vessels

RAIN HAMMERED DOWN SO HARD Neal could barely see the road, even with the wipers on high. He peered through the darkness at a pale, wavering rectangle he was pretty sure was the Shepherd's Point Community Hall. The lights were off. He pulled in front of the building and ran for the door, hoping Miriam had left him a note. The aluminum awning over the entrance amplified the din of downpour. He found a flyer about the meeting she'd invited him to attend, taped inside the door's window facing out, but no note.

A familiar disappointment sank through Neal. That was Miriam, consistent in her changeable ways, what his shrink called her pattern of behavior. Phone after months of silence, arrange a meeting connected to something impersonal, in this case an environmental matter about which he was wholly ignorant, and then turn non-responsive again. "*SAVE OUR COAST,*" the flyer beseeched, "*COASTAL EROSION CAN BE RETARDED.*" Neal frowned at the wording, turned to scan his surroundings. He didn't know if Miriam had gotten his message that his flight had been delayed. If he phoned more than once to find out he'd be accused of crowding her, and he'd used up his quota.

Which was irrelevant because his cell phone didn't have a signal, anyway. He needed a place to stay, now, and he was tired. It was after midnight. The drive from Portland had been an interminable crawl, especially through the hills. Shepherd's Point was a tiny, seaside hamlet. Evidently they didn't keep street lights on past bedtime. The zone illuminated by the rental car's headlights met darkness in all directions.

He rubbed the knobby scar on the side of his face. The old wound ached when it rained. Rubbing didn't help; pain lived at an elusive depth beneath numb skin. He cursed and ran back to the car, reversed into the intersection and turned on the high beams to illuminate the street signs. Hemlock and Crow—it was the Community Hall, all right. He sighed. He was a fool. His shrink was right: He'd made chasing after women who didn't want him his life's work. None had ever run him through his paces like Miriam. Right when he was about to let go, deep inside where it counted, she would show up or call and say or do something that gave him hope. He would believe, again, that he had a chance, and fall over himself trying to please her. He was a fool, casting about to fill a void in his life dimensionless as the night. He was too old. It would be filled with shovel-fulls of dirt.

He studied his map. 'Main Street,' a couple of blocks away, seemed the most likely place to find accommodations. He found the street, drove its five-block stretch of shops, restaurants, small motels and one gas station. Everything was closed up tight, not a candle burning anywhere. He pulled under the port cochère of the Seaside Lodge, found a doorbell labeled 'After Hours,' rang and rang to no avail. He tried the other places with the same result. It occurred to him that the power might be out, and he made the circuit again, pounding on doors. Still no answer. People in this town must be deaf or deep sleepers. He'd have to spend the night in the car.

He drove toward the ocean. He wanted to park where he could hear the surf. That small comfort at least he would have. The thought made him conscious of deeper fatigue. He was ready to let go of wanting and wishing. One of these times would be his last, and his feelings for Miriam would fail in earnest. It saddened him to think she might come to him one day, warm, open, yielding in her attitude, and it might not matter, that it could be too late. He'd been too late himself, before, and knew he was close to his own threshold of disaffection. He didn't want to think about it, just wanted to sleep.

He saw something in the road, hit the brakes and leaned forward, squinting. It looked like a body. Neal stared a moment, pulled ahead slowly and got out. A man—it seemed a man—in a seaman's jacket and jeans, sprawled, face down, near the curb. Neal toed him gently in the thigh and stepped back. "Hey, you all right?" No movement. He squatted and felt for a pulse, found one, groaned with relief. He eased the man onto his back. Boy, rather, brown-haired and dough-faced, maybe fifteen years old. His eyes fluttered open.

"Are you all right?" Neal asked again.

The boy focused on him. His mouth started to form words, but his eyes strained with panic and he shoved Neal away.

"Hey!"

The boy jumped up and ran off left between houses. Neal stood and watched him go. Kid must be drunk. Or high. Who knew what went on in these hills.

Thoroughly soaked, now, Neal got back in the car and drove on, shaking his head. He found a sign that read *Beachside Parking*, pulled into the lot, parked facing the water.

Here he was again, a prodigal returned. This salt had nearly killed him and still it called to his soul. Even now, after all these years, the allure was too great. He'd been right to run away. A corporate cubicle in Sacramento might be dull business but you couldn't drown in it.

He grimaced sourly and nodded to himself: That was his part. He couldn't blame Miriam for her reticence. She would never move inland, and he wouldn't want her to. She would diminish, removed from the sea.

He grew chilled in his wet clothes. He turned on the heater and killed the headlights, listened to invisible waves. He remembered little of the night his boat went down. Gasping for breath, darkness writhing with the churning sea. He woke up retching on the beach, the right side of his face screaming with pain. Later he found the body of one of his crew.

That was where he'd met Miriam, years later in that same place, north of Big Sur where he'd washed ashore. Irresistible impulses drew him back, morbid curiosity large among them. He walked miles of empty beach until he stopped thinking. Seeing and hearing nothing but waves, he became aware of another presence. A woman, naked, dark-haired, striding toward him across the sand. Her beauty shocked him, filled him with sudden breath. She came to him, unaffected and shameless in her nudity, held his gaze. Every element of her presence testified to the naturalness of her state. Before he could speak she touched his scar. Like a prayer answered—the loss hardest to accept—he *felt* it.

"*What happened?*"

"Rogue wave."

She frowned, tilted her head.

"*Capsized my boat. Troll line caught me, tore half my face off. Almost. They sewed it back on.*"

Empathy showed in her eyes. Her hand still held the scar, awakening benumbed flesh. "*My crew drowned.*"

Something from her, like a dust of embers, infiltrated his being, found his wounds—not just the physical ones—and treated them. One touch, and he was hers. He wanted to kiss her until there was nothing left. He never had. They'd danced but they'd never made love.

His shrink said the Miriam in his head wasn't the real Miriam. Eight grand to have his own diagnosis confirmed: He was a fool.

He started to put his seat back when a flash of lightning illuminated the beach. What he saw in the vivid instant banished drowsiness. He turned the headlights back on, switched on the high beams. Through the white veil of rain he made out one of the mounds the lightning had revealed. About a hundred feet away. Neal told himself it was a rock.

He got out, stood behind the door and peered through the rain. It wasn't a rock. He closed the door, stepped over the curb onto the wet sand, stopped, ran. The caution he'd had with the boy was gone. He grabbed the body by its shoulder and pulled it onto its back. The man's eyes and mouth were open, signifying nothing. Other bodies lay nearby, a couple of them lolling in the surf. Neal didn't need to check if they were dead, too. Another lightning flash revealed the horrible truth. Hundreds of bodies lay strewn on the beach, south for at least a quarter of a mile and all the way north to the rocky hook of the point.

Neal backed away, fell, scrambled, tore out of the parking lot and was several blocks away before he slammed on the breaks and slid sideways into the right-hand curb so hard the driver's side wheels lurched off the pavement. He clung to the steering wheel, desperate to keep going. But there was a question he couldn't escape. It was nothing to do with what had happened. He would be a thousand miles away before he cared about that. The thing he couldn't escape was not knowing if Miriam was with the others on that beach.

He swallowed and steadied himself, checked his cell phone. His hand shook so bad he had to put it on the arm rest to read it. No signal.

He wasn't about to risk getting stuck in the sand, driving on that beach. He needed a flashlight. Without thinking about it he turned the car around, stopped again in the middle of the road, took a deep, shuddering breath. Now he knew why no one had answered their doors.

He needed a phone connected to a land line. And a flashlight. He'd have to break in somewhere. Not a house, a business. He remembered a general store, at the end of Main Street near the beach.

Neal drove past art galleries, clothing and novelty shops. The general store had a wood-frame, plate glass door flanked by a display window. Neal aimed his headlights at the storefront, got out and looked for something to use to break in. A series of short pipe posts connected by drooping chains bordered a flower bed between the sidewalk and street. The pairs of posts at the narrow ends of the bed were only connected to each other. Neal kicked one. In the rain-soaked earth it yielded. He worked it loose, then its partner, dragged them by the chain to the door, swung one post by the other into the glass, shattering it. He used the pipe he'd swung with to knock down the jagged perimeter and stepped through.

Something was off. The place smelled like low tide. The lights from his car limned customary aisles of merchandise but the aisles were crisscrossed by streamers of what looked like seaweed. It was all over the floor, too, slimy underfoot. Neal picked a piece up and held it in the light, smelled it. Seaweed. The part of his mind that favored logic served up a flimsy notion of kids pulling a prank. The rest of him, mind, bone and soul, locked on getting the hell gone.

He found a land-line phone behind the service counter. No dial tone. He punched buttons without effect, slammed the handset in the cradle.

He leaned on the counter, head bowed, paused on the prospect of what he was planning to do—search that long stretch of beach for the corpse of the woman he loved. He pictured himself doing it, going from body to body, couldn't help imagining the whole mob coming back to life and eating his brain. Which wasn't as bad as not being able to imagine what put them there. He saw his dead ship-mate, broken in the surf with his mouth full of sand.

Maybe Miriam wasn't dead, though. His time might be as well spent going house to house as combing the beach. Either way he couldn't search effectively on his own. Whatever had happened here needed a massive response. He wouldn't have to drive all the way to Portland, just go back up the highway until he got reception.

He couldn't imagine leaving while there was any possibility that Miriam was alive. At the same time it seemed obvious the greatest chance of saving her lie with involving the authorities. He decided to at least try driving inland a ways to see if he could find cell reception.

He still wanted a flashlight. The counter was in shadow and it was darker behind it but he didn't want to search the aisles. He felt through drawers and shelves under the counter. His hands brushed sharp protrusions he couldn't see. He found a long, heavy flashlight in one of the drawers, turned it on. Barnacles clung to the counter top and the cabinets underneath. The cash register was half covered with them. Some opened when the light hit them.

They were alive.

Movement at the rim of sight made Neal look up. The boy he'd found in the street was outside, watching him from across the small parking lot. Neal had forgotten about him. Something else caught the kid's attention and he bolted. Neal ran out, jumped in the car and went after him. The boy left the sidewalk and ran between buildings again. Neal gunned it and took the corner hard, a short block on spotted the boy running across the next street and again between houses. Neal sped to the next corner, fish-tailed around it. The boy emerged and bounded to the sidewalk before he saw Neal and cut back into the houses. Neal shot forward, stopped and jumped out, ran around the far side of a bungalow, more collided with the boy than caught him. They fell together, Neal on top.

Neal pinned the boy down. "Why are you running? What the hell happened here?"

The boy's face was a blur in the darkness. It sounded like he was trying to say something but it was swallowed by the rain.

"Kid, just tell me." Neal steadied his voice. "I'm not going to hurt you."

"Shih-ih-ih-ih-" the boy stuttered, "shih-ih-ih-ip-wreck!"

There was something wrong with the kid. Neal shined the flashlight at him, saw a scar near his hairline. He was impaired somehow, maybe from an injury. Neal released him and sat back on his haunches. Giving chase had been reflex. He didn't know what he was doing, now. The order of weird in this town was beyond him. He stood up and held out his hand, "Come on."

The boy let Neal help him up but then ran away again.

Neal sighed. "Kid!" He ran after him. "Kid, *wait!*" It was a small chance but the boy knew something that would help Neal find Miriam.

The boy ran inside a two-story stucco house, and left the door open. Neal leapt up the steps and inside but then stopped. It smelled like it had in the general store.

"Kid?"

Neal shined the flashlight around. Sea urchins, barnacles, muscles and anemones grew on the walls, ceiling, sofa, arm chairs, coffee table, entertainment center...there was seaweed everywhere. Neal swallowed. *Kid, come on.*

He heard movement upstairs. Neal crossed the living room, shone the flashlight up a stairway lined with photos and paintings, less colonized by sea life. He climbed, hesitantly. "Goddamit...." A few steps from the upper landing he looked back. Something in one of the photos....

There were pictures of the boy growing up, group shots with his parents. He seemed, like Neal, to be an only child. The boy's father was a fisherman. Several photos showed the two on the deck of a troller, similar to the one Neal had captained. The kid looked sharp and clear-eyed in the photos. Neal identified what had caught his attention, a framed newspaper clipping: "*Survivor Of Fishing Tragedy Found.*" In the picture people on a dock watched a stretcher be lifted off a small cabin ship.

One of the onlookers was Miriam.

A floorboard creaked. Neal turned the flashlight up the stairway. The kid stood at the top, staring at him. He glanced at the framed clipping, looked back at Neal.

"It's all right," Neal said, "I'm not—"

The boy sprang down and pointed at Miriam in the picture.

"She the sea."

Neal stared. "You know her?" He grabbed the boy by his shoulders. "You know this woman? Have you seen her? Where is she?"

"Muh-Muh-Muh-Muh—"

"Miriam."

The boy nodded.

"Where is she?"

The boy wriggled free of Neal's grasp and pointed at Miriam in the picture again. "She the sea."

Neal wasn't sure he wanted to understand. "Are you saying she's on the beach?" He searched the boy's eyes. "With the others?"

The boy was a cipher. He frowned and kept pointing at the picture.

Neal sighed. "Come on, kid, I'm gonna get us out of here."

The boy fell against Neal and wrapped his arms around him.

"All right, all right." Neal worked his way down the stairs with the boy clinging to him. "Ease up. Here, take my hand, take my hand." The boy clutched Neal's hand and Neal led him outside.

The rain had let up. Neal heard the surf. It was close. Beachfront houses lined the opposite side of the street. He took the boy to the car and put him in the back seat. The boy lay down and pulled his jacket over his head.

"Neal," a voice called.

Goosebumps scored Neal's flesh. He whirled, saw a figure across the street, shined the light at it. Miriam was there, staring around like she didn't recognize her surroundings. Awash with relief, Neal ran to her, seized her in his arms. "Oh god, thank god you're alive!"

She did not return his embrace. He released her, shined the light at her again. For an instant her skin seemed translucent. Neal had a fleeting impression of something squirming under the surface. He frowned and shook his head. Her dress, a gauzy, flower-patterned thing completely inappropriate to the weather, hung on her like a wet sock.

"You've got to be freezing. Come on, let's get you out of here." He reached for her arm.

She pulled away. "I'm not leaving."

"What? Miriam!"

She strode toward the ocean.

"Where are you going?"

"You don't have to stay, Neal. You should go." She tossed him a pouty, petulant look over her shoulder, like she did when she wanted attention. It was an oddly adolescent wile of hers that had always struck Neal as playful. Now it was grotesque.

He started after her but the boy grabbed his sleeve and tugged on it, pleading, "No!"

Neal pulled free and ran after Miriam. Something was wrong with her. She ran, too, between flat-roofed cottages, laughing as she went. The kid caught up with Neal and tried again to stop him.

Halfway across the beach, Miriam turned to face Neal. He freed himself again from the boy, but when he was about twenty feet from Miriam something else stopped him.

He shone the flashlight around. The bodies were gone. There were other things, oval objects of some kind....

The clouds broke around a gibbous moon and its light poured through. The objects were human heads. The bodies had been buried in the sand with their heads exposed, all facing the sea in neat rows.

Miriam stood among them, smiling at Neal like a mischievous artist amid an exhibit of her works. She must be in shock, he thought. But a force burst from her, unmistakably *from her*, that hit Neal like a gale of dread.

"Miriam...."

Power poured from her like a rising sea. Her smile and gaze turned inward, as if, in a helpless, distracted way, she poised for a moment upon some irony.

She turned her head and lifted her chin, directing Neal's attention down the beach to his left. Things he hadn't seen by lightning flash, with the dead seizing notice, he saw now—stacks of big pipes, of the kind used to redistribute slurry, and a dredge ship lying on its side out in the water.

Miriam watched him, waiting to see his reaction. He was caught in the field of her power, unable to escape understanding that this was all her doing, an accomplishment she wanted to share with him. Like a cat leaving a mouse by his bed. It scalded his mind, how terribly he had misunderstood her.

She let her dress fall to the sand and came to him, naked, as when they first met. God, she was beautiful. The boy cowered behind Neal. Miriam reached to touch Neal's face but hesitated, saw in his eyes that he no longer wanted her gift. Her touch penetrated his wound again, but this time amplified pain.

Neal flinched away. Tears slipped from his eyes. He backed up a step, straightened and stood his ground. He would not go down cowering. For the first time he saw uncertainty in Miriam. She had not expected this break between them, didn't want to accept that they couldn't go back from what she had done here. He couldn't reassure her. She would know it was a lie.

She went to the water. He did not follow. Calf-deep in the surf, she turned and faced him for the last time. He thought he saw a flicker of regret cross her brow but it could have been fantasy. She fell apart into what she was, something not human that never had a name.

The boy pulled on Neal's arm.

The creature Miriam became swept a tentacled pincer at the heads on the beach. "They meant to deny me," she said, in a cavernous voice. Which had nothing to do with anything. Or maybe it did. But she was covering her disappointment. He had hurt her.

She pointed at the boy, and in her eyes, which had multiplied and become many, Neal read a mimicry of concern.

"I'll take care of him," he said. He could favor her illusions.

She nodded, and released him. Like a nightmare lost upon waking, she fell apart entirely.

Neal couldn't see the wave but he felt its sub-audible rumble. He ran back to the car with the boy, tore east toward the highway. The boy curled up on the seat beside him, whimpering.

"Don't look back, kid."

Her wave would take the town and the dead. He would never tell anyone what he had seen. He didn't want to talk about anything, ever again.

Knowing her nature wasn't the worst thing, nor what she'd done. She'd shown him what he was, what they all were, under the skin, where it hurt. But that wasn't the worst thing, either.

He still loved her. He couldn't help it.

Stephen T. Vessels was nominated for the 2014 International Thriller Award, and is a recipient of the Santa Barbara Writers conference award for Best Fiction. His stories have appeared in Ellery Queen's Mystery Magazine and Grey Matter Press' Equilibrium Overturned, and his collection, The Mountain and the Vortex, will be released next year by Muse Harbor. He has just completed an SF novel, "Fall of the Messengers." Poems he composed in his own invented forms have been published in literary journals and in a chapbook by Slack Buddha Press. He is also a visual artist, has exhibited his paintings and drawings in galleries and group shows, and has written art reviews for the Santa Barbara Independent. Two years ago he started drawing with the same implement he writes with, a Uni-ball pen, and has produced over 400 drawings in that medium. In his spare time he listens to music by obscure and forgotten composers.

The Jinn Master

Cynthia Ray

MARINA STOOD ON THE PORCH of her dilapidated trailer and watched Eddy get out of his pick-up. Puffs of dust rose up where his feet hit the ground as he walked towards her. She took a deep breath and put her hands on her hips, "So where were you last night?"

He put his hands up, "Relax babe. Ran into Bob and the boys at the Pair-A-Dice Lounge. Played cards all night."

Marina frowned. "Pair-A-Dice? Ain't that where Lucinda works?"

Eddy shook his head, "Forget about that." He reached into his jeans pocket and pulled out a small black velvet box. "Look. I got you a present."

In spite of her anger, Marina was intrigued. Eddy was out of work, and money. Maybe he'd won some money at cards last night. She smiled and breathed a sigh of relief. Great. He could finally pay her the money he'd borrowed. The bill collectors were getting to her, and she didn't know how long she could put them off.

Eddy climbed the porch stairs and pressed the box into her hand. "Go on, babe, open it."

Marina ran her finger across the soft black velvet of the tiny jewelry box. When she lifted the lid, a faint smell of mustiness and mothballs made her cough. There on the yellowed silk lay a tarnished silver ring set with a small green stone.

"What the hell is this, Eddy?"

He beamed at her. "A wishing ring." He pushed a paper towards her. "See, it's got a genuine Jinni inside. I got it on eBay."

Marina glanced at the paper and saw the price. $199.00 plus shipping. She snapped the box shut and in a low, quiet voice asked, "Where did you get the money for this, Eddy?"

He crossed his arms and lifted his chin. "Hey, it's a gift. Why do you need to know?" He tried to push past her into the trailer but she put her arm across the door.

"Eddy, did you use my credit card to pay for this?"

He shrugged. "I thought you could wish for money, then pay everything off. " He pointed to the ring. "That should cover whatever I owe you…."

The blood pounded in her temples like a drum and sweat trickled down her neck. Her body convulsed in anger and she threw the jewelry box into the yard. What a moron. What a fool. No. She was the idiot. She'd let him move in with her again; she'd given him money, lots of money; she…well. It ended here. Marina yelled so loud the rusty door shook. "Get. Out. NOW."

Eddy backed up a step. "Whoa, babe. You don't want to do this. Calm down."

Marina stomped into the house and yanked open the nightstand. She pulled out a gun and pulled off the safety. She heard him come into the living room, and she stood at the bedroom door and pointed the gun at him. His eyes widened and he put his hands up again. "Shit, put that thing down, babe. You're scarin' me."

She laughed in a high-pitched gulp, then sobbed, then laughed. "Get out, Eddy, and don't come back or I will shoot you. I swear to God."

She lifted the gun and shot over his head. The ceiling lamp shattered and fell around his head. Eddy moved faster than she'd ever seen him move. He jumped into the truck and pulled out in a whoosh of gravel, dust and screeching tires.

Marina cursed. She'd messed up her ceiling, her lamp and made a huge mess. Screw him! She threw the gun down and grabbed the football lamp and ripped the cord from the wall. She opened the door and threw it onto the lawn. It hit the ground with a satisfying crash of glass. She'd always hated that thing.

She threw his clothes, his porn movies, and his beer signs into piles on the lawn, then fell into a chair, exhausted. Why did she always choose such low-life losers? Why? Because she was a loser. A broke, broken down, hard luck loser.

She rummaged through her medicine cabinet looking for her Valium. She gulped the last tablet and gripped the sink. As she stared at her wan face, she thought of the ring. She'd paid for it; maybe she could get her money back from eBay. She went into the yard and dug through the pile of trashy belongings until she found the black box skootched up against the wire fence post.

Back in the trailer, Marina poured herself a glass of Chardonnay from the box in the refrigerator and sat down at the battered Formica table. Her hands were still shaking from the altercation with Eddy. She put the box on the table and thought about wishes.

If there were such a thing, she would wish the damn bill collectors into the deepest pit of hell. She hated them harassing her day and night—threatening to take her house. Okay, technically it was a trailer, and not much of one, but it was home. Then she would wish for money, buckets of money. She'd go to school and maybe learn to do medical coding, or art. She'd buy a really sweet little house on the other side of town, near the river. She daydreamed about sitting on her patio, overlooking the river, breathing in the smell of wisteria and jasmine.

Yup. Her life was a wreck and she needed an intervention—stat. Money. Yes, immediately, if not sooner, to take the pressure off. Next, a new fun job with a good boss, not the sleazebag she reported to now who groped her every time she walked by. And better yet, wouldn't it be nice to have a boyfriend who treated her right?

She took a sip of wine, then ran her finger across the soft black velvet of the tiny jewelry box. She scowled at the thought of gullible, stupid Eddie buying this idiotic piece of crap ring for her, as if that could make up for all of his cheating and lying. And of all the nerve. Buying it with her money. Never mind all that. He was history.

She opened the box and put the ring on. She read the blurb that came with the ring. This modest stone was supposed to hold 2342 year-old Jinn. The eBay ad said so. She laughed, tipped her wine glass up and finished it off. Sure! She'd try it for a laugh. She rubbed the stone, turning the ring on her finger and chanted the words as the blurb instructed.

"O Great Jinn, I, the owner of this ring, command thee to appear." She held her breath and waited. Nothing. She hadn't expected anything to happen, but some part of her was disappointed. Perhaps the ring seemed a little warmer on her finger, but perhaps not.

As she poured another glass of wine, the sound of jangling bells startled her. A pungent odor of musk and stale sweat filled the room, followed by a swirling, billowing cloud of white cigar smoke. She winced and gagged. "What the hell?"

When the smoke cleared, a slight man with thinning brown hair that stuck out around his ears stood before her. He had uneven yellow teeth, a small potbelly, a caved in chest and stood naked except for a pair of red silk shoes that curled up at the toes.

The Jinn gripped the edge of the table and shook his head, then sat down across from her. He put his head in his hands and groaned.

Marina furrowed her brow in disbelief. "*You're* the Jinn of the Ring?"

The man snorted and looked up at her with rheumy eyes, "That's me alright." He stood up, still holding on to the table and gave a slight bow. "I apologize, but appearing after such a long lock down always makes me nauseous." He pointed at the ring and gave a weary sigh, "I suppose you are my new Mistress?"

Marina shook her head. He didn't look like much of a Jinni, and he smelled funny. She looked away from his skinny nakedness, embarrassed. He reminded her of nothing more than a plucked chicken. Exactly the kind of Jinn she would get. IF he was real. Had to be a hallucination; she shouldn't mix wine and Valium. But he smelled real enough.

He sat down again and looked around, "Do you mind if I smoke?"

"Uh, I guess not," she stammered and watched in amazement as he pulled a cigar from behind his ear and lit it. She wrapped her sweaty hands around her glass of wine. She wondered if Jinn's drank wine.

She stared at his age spotted face in disgust. Why did everything she did turn to shit? Dammit. She took a deep breath and decided she would have to make the best of the situation. Any Jinn was better than no Jinn, right? Maybe he could grant a wish or two.

"Would you like a glass of chardonnay?" she asked as she made her way to the refrigerator to refill her own glass. She filled it all the way to the top and sipped a little off the top of the glass to keep it from spilling over the edge.

The Jinn took a puff of his cigar, "Nah, I'm more of a scotch whiskey kind of guy. You wouldn't happen to have any would you?" He looked at her hopefully.

Marina dug through her cupboards until she unearthed a dusty half-empty bottle of peach brandy left over from a cooking experiment. It was old, but these things didn't go bad, did they? She poured a plastic tumbler full of the amber liquid and handed it to him. He tasted it and grimaced.

He stood up and bowed again. "Forgive my rudeness. My name is Khalid. Formerly known as Khalid the Munificent, First Jinn of all the Western Realms." He patted his chest and smiled.

She averted her eyes and blushed, "Nice to meet you, um, Mr. Khalid. I'm Marina. Would you mind putting on a robe or something?"

He looked down. "Oops, sorry." He vanished for a few moments and returned dressed in a wrinkled black and white caftan that smelled of mothballs. He gave her a toothy grin, "Better?"

He took another puff from the cigar and looked into her eyes. "I am required to serve and obey the owner of the ring, whoever and whatever that may be. I am your slave."

Marina's mouth gaped. Wow. This sounded more like it. Excitement coursed through her veins and her hand shook, spilling wine.

Khalid pointed to the ring on her finger. "My spirit was bound to that ring by an evil sorceress whom I had angered." He paused, lost in thought, and then said, "In retrospect, it would have been better to have left the slave girls alone." He bit on the cigar, and grimaced around it. "One mistake and Bam! I'm a slave, forever, to the whims and wishes of humans. Do you know what that means, Marina?" He didn't wait for an answer. "No? I'll tell you."

He gripped the plastic tumbler. "It means I live in the between world, waiting. Always waiting. I can never initiate actions on my own behalf, nor pursue my own interests. And when I am called, I must appear immediately. I must obey whatever human has come into command of the ring, no matter how inane their commands might be."

Marina stared at him, openmouthed. She felt a twinge of sympathy for him. She felt like a slave to her job, too, but this talk made her uncomfortable. They should be discussing her wishes and desires, not his problems with his ex. Besides, if he cheated on her like that, she couldn't blame the woman for locking him in a ring. What an idiot.

He took another sip of brandy and grimaced. "There is a way out." He set the tumbler down and reached for her hand across the table. He squeezed it and she pulled away and put her hands in her lap. He drummed his fingers on the table then locked eyes with her. "You could, of your own free will, release me of this bond."

She squirmed under his gaze, and then a flush of anger spread across her chest and made her cheeks warm. How dare he ask her that? The eBay blurb said nothing about this kind of thing. Was he trying to trick her out of her rights because she was an inexperienced Jinn Master? He thought she was a loser and could take advantage of her. Well, that wasn't going to happen. She glared at him. She would command him to shut up and get on with the business at hand.

It was all too much; Eddy the lying cheat, the creditors calling day and night, the letters threatening to repossess this dilapidated trailer, the boss that pressured her day after day to perform 'favors' for him. It was too much and it had to end. The Jinn could be the answer to all of this. Her way out. Absolutely no way would she allow him to cheat her out of her rights.

She took in his thinning hair; his sad eyes, his tobacco stained teeth. She didn't need this crazy old coot around for long. Let him grant her a few wishes and then she would release him, and upgrade to the deluxe version. Yes, a handsome Jinn with six-pack abs and white teeth. And decent clothes. What was up with that moldy caftan?

She cleared her throat and forced a smile. "Mr. Khalid, here is my offer. After granting me the three customary wishes, I will certainly release you." She felt gracious, magnanimous.

He bit on his cigar. "I'm sorry. It doesn't work that way. If I grant any of your wishes I must continue on in the cycle. You have to release me now...or never."

Tears sprang to her eyes and she blinked them back. "But I need...I mean...."

The Jinn twirled his cigar between his thumb and forefinger, knocking ashes off onto the floor. His eyes watered. "I have served hundreds of humans, and not one has granted my request or I would not stand here before you now. It's always the same. Money, riches, power. A new car, a beautiful lover, a big mansion, more money, revenge against ones enemies, more money. Always the same." He waved his cigar at her. "Do you know how damn depressing that is?"

He stood up and paced back and forth in front of the table, his caftan swirling behind him, stirring the smell of mothballs and sweat upward. "Of course, who could blame them? It's impossible to have the seeming answer to all your prayers, to all your desires, standing before you and then turn away and return to a life without hope. I fall into the hands of the desperate."

He shook his head and frowned, "Perhaps all humans are desperate." He pointed a gnarled finger at her. "Do you think anyone ever asked for an end to war? For an end to poverty and disease? The cure for cancer? Ha! Greedy buggers."

She gritted her teeth as waves of guilt washed over her. She was as selfish and greedy as the rest. Well, maybe one of her wishes should be to end poverty for everyone. Why not? It was a miserable way to live.

She beheld the depths of sadness written in Khalid's eyes and clenched her jaw and ground her teeth. Why, of all the cursed Jinns, did she end up with this one? Stupid Eddy. Stupid eBay. She burst into tears, put her head down on the table and tried to think.

She needed money, dammit. She was on a fast track to bankruptcy and losing her trailer. The cable was cut off last month; the electricity was next. Her love life, if it could be called that, stank. Eddy had wrecked her car and maxed out her credit cards. Her job was a weight around her neck. She woke up every day with what felt like heavy stones sitting on her chest, barely able to breathe or move, afraid of what new humiliations the day would bring.

Still, she felt sorry for this tawdry Jinni. He reminded her of the abandoned kittens mewing on the porch with their hungry cries. For Gods sake, he reminded her of herself, slave to circumstances, slave to others desires. This is *not* what she had bargained for.

Goddamnit. She clenched and unclenched her fists as her mind roiled. She hated him for asking for this, and she hated herself for wanting what she wanted. A light bulb went off in her head and she had an inspiration. If she ended poverty, that should include her as well. That would kill two birds with one stone as the old cliché said. She blinked away her tears and asked, "What if I asked for an end to poverty?"

The Jinn blew a smoke ring over her head and sighed, "No, I only used that as an example. I can't really end war or poverty. Unfortunately, my powers are limited. I can only attend to one human will at a time. Your choice remains. To release me of my obligation to you, or to command me as your slave."

Marina cursed under her breath. How unfair to be forced to choose between all that she wanted, no…needed and freeing this very unpleasant Jinn from a curse. Life sucked.

He ignored her and drank his peach brandy and smoked his cigar, seemingly resigned to whatever she chose. She sat up, sniffed and wiped her nose on her sleeve. She wasn't a bad person. She knew what it felt like to be chained to a job, to live without choices. Dammit. She couldn't inflict that on him in good conscience. She groaned. "Okay, what if I let you go? Then what?"

Khalid's face lit up like a can of lighter fluid on a hot barbecue. He pushed his hands through his graying hair and his mouth lifted in a hopeful grin. In a trembling voice he said, "I would be free from the curse—I would no longer be required to dwell in the between world. I could live again. Free." He held his palms towards her, "And you, well, you would receive my grateful and eternal thanks."

Her voice rose, "What good are your thanks when the bill collectors call? What good are your 'eternal thanks' when they repossess my home? What good are your thanks when I lose my job because I refuse to sleep with the bullshit boss?"

Khalid winced. "Look, I know it's tough. Here's what I can do for you. If you release me from bondage, I will stick around and give you advice."

"Advice? Advice? That's it?" She snorted.

"Believe me, I've witnessed a thousand like you ruin their lives. I can give you a few tips." He threw his head back and laughed, then coughed until he turned red.

Marina squeezed her eyes shut. If she released him, she wouldn't be any worse off than before—except for the price of the ring. And she could return it to eBay. It did say there was a 30-day money back guarantee. With a heavy heart, she opened her eyes and murmured, "I may be a fool, but I will release you, Khalid."

He stood up, knocked the chair aside and hugged her. "You won't be sorry."

"Ha, I'm already sorry." Marina sniffed and pushed him away.

"Okay before we do this, let me get my stuff." He vanished then returned with a trunk and a worn velvet bag tied with a rope. He set them on the floor and turned to her. He beamed, and rocked on his silk-shod feet. "I can't believe it! You are one special human being."

Marina gritted her teeth, "Special-Smecial. Let's get this over with."

He took her hands in his and slipped the ring off her finger. He put it in her hand and kissed her forehead. "My dear Marina. You are as beautiful and radiant as an enchanted full moon on a summer night."

Blushing, she stepped back. Khalid instructed her, "Lift up the ring, and repeat these words three times,

'Be free O Jinn of this Ring!

Of my own free will

I do release you from your bonds.'

With a sigh she lifted the ring up above her head and closed her eyes. The first time she intoned the words, the ring grew heavier in her grasp. The second time she chanted the verse, the ring vibrated and turned so hot in her hand she almost dropped it. The third time, when she exclaimed, "I do release you from your bonds" the ring shattered and fell into pieces on the floor. An electric, sizzling smell of ozone filled the air and she blinked and looked at the Jinn.

He trembled, with tears in his eyes. He tried to speak but no words came. He knelt in front of her and clasped her legs. Sobs wracked his body and he prostrated himself before her. Embarrassed, she lifted him up.

Khalid wiped his eyes on his sleeve and laughed. "I am so happy." He knelt before the trunk and lifted the lid. He reached in and pulled out a canvas bag and handed it to Marina. He waved to her to open it.

She pulled it open and nearly dropped it in surprise. It was full of jewels and gold and silver coins. "What…what is this?"

Khalid dropped into the chair, sipped the peach brandy. "A reward. A token of my appreciation. I couldn't mention that or your pledge to free me would have been tainted and invalid." He beamed at her. "And, as promised, I will advise you on how to invest this money, and many other things besides. It was a lucky day when you called me from the ring, and released me, O beneficent one."

She ran to him and kissed him on the cheek. His skin felt warm and raspy on her lips. Tears ran down her face. "Khalid, thank you. You've saved my life."

He put his hand on her head, "And you've saved mine." He stood up, walked to the sink and poured the peach brandy down the drain. "I want to celebrate. We're going to find a liquor store and buy a decent bottle of scotch." He pointed to her glass of wine. "My first bit of advice for you is to switch to Champagne."

She put her hands on her hips and said, "Fine. But I have some advice for you as well."

Khalid lifted his eyebrows as she continued, "You can't be seen in public in that ridiculous caftan. And when was the last time you had a shower?" She walked over and took the cigar from his lips and stubbed it out on a saucer. She smiled at him. "The cigars will have to go."

Cynthia Ray lives and writes short fiction in Vancouver, Washington (the *other* Vancouver). She is a priest and a spiritual feminist. She believes in possibility—the possibility of creating a world where a person's value doesn't hang on what they own, the color of their skin, their gender or any other outer thing. Her short stories have appeared in Fringe Magazine, Sorcerous Signals, Anthropomorphic Podcasts, Apokrupha Press Dark Bits Anthology and Pendragon's Memory of Dragons Anthology.

True Colors

Pamela Jean Herber

ELISSA WOUND UP HER VOICE and then forced it out in long even breaths to match the high pitched wail of the braking freight train. Ever since she could remember, the eerie sounds of the freight yard had called her out here to sit next to the tracks. She was far enough away from Maryanne and the other elders to not be noticed—for her voice to blend in with the real scene in this human place.

She was waiting for Jake. He had been coming here regularly since he moved to the shelter home a few blocks away. Every day he moved a little closer to the tracks and every day he stayed a little longer. Elissa knew his day was coming. Her day was coming. She had first noticed him before he even arrived at her spot among the daisies. His voice had carried out over the dusty gravel street and across the litter-filled vacant lot to her ears.

As Jake had walked closer, his voice had grown bigger and turned into the shape of a song. "Wait for me, you'll see me here again," he sang. Elissa's ears stood at attention. Another sound to harmonize with. Even though Jake's voice was deeper and rougher than hers, she could pull it off. If she was subtle enough. That first attempt and then all during her first meeting with Jake, she whispered the words, the individual sounds barely distinguishable as song. None of the elders had marched down to scold her. Maryanne had not stirred from her sleep. Each day, Elissa became braver and pushed up the volume just a little. Each day, her voice claimed more of the song. Each day, Jake's voice softened almost imperceptibly.

Today she noticed that Jake was turning gray and translucent. The first day he had dragged himself out here, there had been color in him. Elissa had seen it and had fantasized about taking it home with her; about pulling all the color out of his sick old body and wrapping it into a compact bundle. If she folded it into just the right shape and fastened it to her being securely, she might get away with it. She still had plenty of Wite-Out to blend it in. Maryanne seemed to be more than willing to give her as much of the stuff as she asked for. Even more, sometimes, than she needed. Maryanne was happy with Elissa as long as all that showed of her was white. Elissa tugged at her lip until it threatened to crack. A hint of pink revealed the existence of the blood that flowed beneath. She had better get back before Maryanne woke from her midday nap.

MARYANNE WAS flowing white silk over ice. Sometimes her knees stuck involuntarily together on her way from her bleached velour sofa to the refrigerator for a glass of skim milk. A few weeks ago, Elissa had interrupted her on one of those journeys to the kitchen.

"Maryanne? Today, when I was chipping at my nail polish, instead of ordinary white, I found the palest blue and even a little purple underneath." What Elissa hadn't said was that sometimes light flashed from the under-layer like a diamond just caught by the sun. Most of the time, she only found pink flesh. But even pastel pink was not white. Maryanne had pulled a little bottle of Wite-Out from under her sleeve and slipped it secretively to Elissa. From that day, if a little color showed through, Maryanne would gently remind her to add another coat of Wite-Out. But, oh my god, if the sapphire blue caught her eye, a look of panic would attack Maryanne's whole body and her bright white would turn stark against a suddenly black room. Elissa would blot the frightful patch of color with racing hands and stand with a quivering lip until she had flooded the spot, the eyesore, the defect, with enough of the stuff to drown a small dog.

The sapphire and the amethyst hadn't shown themselves in quite some time. Elissa never knew quite where they might be floating around inside, unless they moved. She listened very carefully for those inner journeys and recorded where they stopped. An extra coat of Wite-Out would do the trick as long as she didn't miss the next motion. Sometimes she felt like a patchwork quilt that no one could recognize as such. She wondered if any of the others felt like that; little pieces all stitched together to hold the stuffing in. Some pieces getting old and dry and cracking and others still wet and new.

Maryanne had warned Elissa about the colors sapphire and amethyst.

She said, "Those colors are lies. They are only temptations fabricated by the grays to make us weak and to convince us to fall. They want us to become like them. The beaten."

"But Maryanne, they aren't beaten. They keep coming back. All we do is sit around and watch them until they run out of gas," Elissa said.

"I didn't hear you say that, young lady. Do you understand? You never said anything of the kind. Our conversation is over."

"But…." She wanted to tell Maryanne about the day she saw the boy on the river. That day, the boy had looked like a Raggedy Andy doll as his body bounced along the rocks down the rapids. Elissa's terror had torn free and turned into a scream. "Don't die! Please don't die!" The boy finally came to rest along the shore where the river spread out and deepened. Elissa ran down to him. She pulled his broken body up onto the grass. He looked to be fifteen or sixteen years old. Elissa's age. Blood trickled from a gash above his left eye and down past his ear. It matted into his sandy-colored hair. What looked like bone was jutting out from his shredded jeans. The boy moaned a little and then all of the colors rushed out of him. Fiery blood turned blue and then to charcoal. His yellow shirt turned the color of wet sand. His face threatened to disappear completely.

"Who are you?" he said. "An angel. I'm sure of it!" He smiled as the last of the green in his eyes twinkled her way. "It's okay, you know," he said.

"You hear me. You see me." Elissa stopped and then started again. "My, uh, name, uh, is Elissa…Are you dead?"

Elissa hadn't seen the cloud of grays approaching. The group overtook the both of them with the smell of honey and the warmth of a bowl of chicken soup. The individual grays were hard to make out, each one blending in with the other. Some more defined than others. Somewhere in the middle and getting closer was a gray with arms and legs and hair. As he came nearer, Elissa could see that his hair was red and his eyes blue. Color! She thought he was coming to greet her but he passed right by her to the dying boy. All that was left of the boy now was a fine mist and an outline. The red-headed gray reached out and mixed his hands with where the boy's had been.

He said, "Welcome home. May you find the strength and the healing that I have found here." He lay down where that boy had been. Then the grays left with the boy and drifted back to their side of the river.

"Good-bye." Elissa said. She had no longer been able to distinguish the broken boy from any of the other gray figures. So, she had just waved at no one in particular in the direction of the group.

THE MINUTE hand on Elissa's wristwatch moved forward as the second-hand clicked past twelve. Ten-forty a.m. Would she ever get out of here? Maryanne was sitting much too close to her on the sofa. Elissa pulled away a few inches, trying not to appear rude. Maryanne's frosted lips closed in on Elissa's face and she thought for a moment that Maryanne was going to kiss her. Instead, she glanced around the room and said, "I had a talk with a friend of mine who knows of these things. I never told you this, but I had a problem similar to yours when I was a girl. This friend of mine, she cured me.

Look, I will show you." She picked up a nail file off of the coffee table and sawed it into her forearm.

"What are you doing!" Elissa grabbed the nail file. "What's the matter with you!"

Maryanne said, "I'm fine. It's fine…Look…See." Her arm looked like a piece of chalk with a chip out of it. Maryanne rubbed her hand over the wound until the chip blended in with the rest of her arm. "See. Not a speck of color to be found."

Elissa rubbed her eyes. Maybe, if she rubbed hard enough, what she had just seen would seem okay. "You're going to do that to me?"

"There's no need to be afraid, dear. Believe me. It's painless."

"When?" Elissa said.

"I have arranged for my friend to be here at eleven o'clock." Mary-anne placed her icy fingers on Elissa's arm. "In twenty minutes. You must never tell anyone."

Elissa scanned the room looking for an escape hatch. Twenty minutes. "What about your nap? Don't you need your nap? You always take your nap at eleven o'clock." And then, "I better go get ready. I better put on something special for the occasion. I'll be right back."

"That's a good girl. That's my Elissa." Maryanne smiled the biggest, hardest grin Elissa had ever seen on her.

Elissa tried not to run to her bedroom and she tried not to slam the door. She failed at both. However, she was successful at opening the window without a sound. And she was successful at jumping out of it with the gentlest swoosh. But then she forgot to watch where her feet landed. As she came down, her foot slipped on a rock or a twig or something. She fell with a thud.

"Damn!" The word jumped out before she could stop it. All she could do now was run. It was ten-fifty. Ten more minutes.

Elissa stopped at her patch of daisies six feet from the railroad tracks. She took three deep breaths. She had to calm down. Jake would be here soon, but not soon enough.

"What time is it?" she said aloud to a grasshopper poised on a nearby blossom. "Don't fly away yet, Hoppy. Stay with me until Jake arrives. I heard that he is right on the edge; that he is scheduled to go over at eleven a.m. Right here. This morning. It's coming around to eleven o'clock within a couple minutes now." She looked back in the direction of the house. Maryanne was creaking out of the door. Thank God she was slow.

Elissa spied Jake pacing toward the tracks. She could feel the heaviness in the air. Jake appeared to be measuring each step to exactly 30 inches. A group of grays floated towards him from the other side of the tracks. The determination and steadiness of Jake's approach sharply contrasted with the excited voices of the grays. Elissa stood waiting until Jake reached the piece of solid ground right next to her. A whistle blew down the track. It blew again and again, turning from a warning to a demand. Jake didn't seem to hear it. As the train drew closer, Jake crouched, placing one leg behind the other for leverage. Elissa did the same. Now she could feel the weight of the train moving the earth. She could smell the metal and grease and power of the thing. Jake was looking straight into the eyes of the engineer. The engineer smiled.

Elissa was so stunned by that smile that she almost didn't see Jake push himself towards the train. He almost slipped through her hands. She wrapped her arms around his solid form just in time and tumbled down with him. She felt icicles latch onto her shoulders. Maryanne. Maryanne's screams mimicked the train's as it hit. They were all pounded onto the tracks and pushed a quarter of a mile before the train stopped. Jake's body was ripped and bloody. Elissa had turned to purple mist. She couldn't tell where Jake ended and she began.

Maryanne's screams crumbled in the air and blew off into the wind. They changed from howling coyotes to fluttering butterfly wings and then to silence. Her body was carried off as if by those butterfly wings. As she floated up and over Whitetown, Maryanne turned into a hologram. Just before the vision of her disappeared, it cracked and shattered, spreading shards of white into the air. The midday sun melted them into a rain that sprinkled down on the little community. Tiny droplets trickled onto the pale skin and long flowing gowns of the whites. Rays of color shone out from the tracks of the droplets.

Elissa held onto Jake. She could feel his life changing places with hers. His body turning to mist and hers to a sturdy human form. "Jake. Stay with me. Show me how to do this. Teach me how to live."

"I can't. I got to leave while I still can. See? My friends are here."

Elissa gripped his soul tighter and then let it go. The cloud of grays gathered around the two of them and then drifted away, carrying Jake. He was gone. She was alone at the side of the tracks. The sun burned red on her skin.

And then, that familiar deep voice came drifting back. "Wait for me, you'll see me here again."

Elissa echoed with her own. Her voice carried the colors of rubies and emeralds and sapphires. "I'll wait for you, you'll see me here again."

Pamela Jean Herber explores the realms of uncertainty. Characters venture into worlds where the differences between right and wrong are tangled, where her characters must tease out the knots to discern the best threads to follow. Sometimes, they succeed. Sometimes, they walk into doom out of sheer frustration. Always, they face an enemy they don't understand.

Five Tips for Outsmarting Satan— and Your Students

Sarina Dorie

TIP NUMBER ONE: KEEP IN MIND *that when you say things like, "I would trade my immortal soul for a full-time teaching job," Satan just might take you up on that offer.*

Looking back, I knew it would be a rough semester. From the start, it made me suspicious a thirty-five year old woman would "retire" from her position as an orchestra teacher in a high school midyear. But when you're only working mornings as a middle school music teacher and subbing in subjects like trigonometry and special education in the afternoon (neither of which you know anything about) you tend not to ask too many questions.

It didn't make me feel a whole lot better when I met with the principal of South Drainfield High to discuss the job.

"I'm concerned that I wouldn't be able to arrive by 12:10 p.m. when my first class would start here at the high school," I said. "My classes at Emerson Middle School end at noon."

The principal pursued her weathered lips, making her face resemble a prune more than a middle-aged woman who frequented tanning beds. "Yes, well, human resources said we had to give you a lunch break and include travel time."

I glanced over the photos on the wall of the principal drinking in bars. In them she wore low cut dresses and mini skirts that I would never as a professional have been caught wearing in public. I refocused my attention. "Oh, that's nice. What time does class start?"

"Hmmph. We wanted to give you three afternoon classes and a study hall, but the district said we had to give you a prep period." She tossed back her highlighted hair, her jowls jiggling—giving me an opportunity to see what happened to cheerleaders at fifty. "So class will start at 1:00 p.m. for you. You should feel grateful. We didn't give a prep to the last music teacher."

"Oh, I see. Uh, thank you." I quickly calculated that in my mind. It would take five minutes to get there, ten minutes on average to find a parking spot at that time of day, five more minutes to walk over to the campus, and half an hour for a lunch break. That left me with a ten minute prep period. Right. How gracious of them. Those were my union dues at work.

It could have been worse, I reminded myself. Anything was better than getting drooled on and clawed at by out-of-control trig students. Oh, and the special ed students too. Almost anything, I soon realized.

After I met the English teacher next to the music room, I suspected things could get far, far worse.

I INTRODUCED myself to the other teachers in the English wing. Mr. Johnson complained how loud the last orchestra teacher was and that the school had no right to put a music class in the same area where *learning* was going on. Mrs. Cleveland bustled around a messy desk, frantically looking for something, telling me she didn't have time to talk. Ms. Peters told me I had to be careful not to let more than one student leave the classroom at once because all they wanted to do was have sex in the bathroom. Eew.

Mr. Frost was a tall, thin man with long black hair and a pointed goatee. He resembled a Spanish poet in his all black attire more than an English teacher.

Since his room was next to mine, I figured it would be convenient to go to him in case I had questions. He sat at a tidy metal desk, staring up at the ceiling and muttering to himself in a deep voice as I came in to introduce myself. "Care…mare…where…hair…fair."

"Hello," I said, hating to interrupt. "I'm Ms. Katy Dunn. I'm your new neighbor."

"Blast it all!" He looked me up and down with an air of bored indifference. "Oh, yes, the new music teacher. I suppose if you have any problems, you can come to me for assistance. You might as well not even bother with the administration. They didn't do much for the last music teacher, even when the students threatened to kill her dog.

"And watch out for that Jamari White. If I were you, I'd get Gabriella Martinez to cough on his desk. She's recovering from mono. Better yet, have her sit next to him and pay her to cough on him. And a little tip, stickers and candy are nothing to these little monsters. Just like inmates, cigarettes are their currency."

I laughed, but stopped when I saw he wasn't smiling. "You're joking, right?"

He stared at me with pale blue eyes, the icy azure unnatural against his swarthy complexion. "You might want to join the other teachers for the 'Friday at Four' at the local bars to de-stress at the end of the week. Though, personally, I prefer my cocktail of Prozac, cocaine and gin. Have fun." He went back to staring at the ceiling and muttering to himself. "Chair…beware…share…dare…share…. Oh, damn it, I just said that one. I don't suppose you might know a good rhyme for the line 'filled with despair'?"

"Um, sorry, no." I slowly backed away, hoping to plan the lessons for my new classes that would start on Monday.

He strummed his fingers against the metal desk. "I would sell my soul to be able to come up with a good rhyme—if I had a soul. Such a pity, isn't it?"

An icy prickle skated down my spine. Something definitely

wasn't right about this school, Mr. Frost being the worst of it.

Tip Number Two: Never show emotion. Especially not fear. These little demons smell weakness and are better at spotting someone's tell than a professional gambler.

If you find teaching rewarding and have a good relationship with your students, it doesn't matter if the administration sucks or the other teachers in your wing are weirdos. It's supposed to be about the joy of music, the dedication to the students; my true reason for teaching. That's how it was for me at the middle school.

I soon learned teaching at a high school was different. On my first day, one of my students peed in the trash can when I wasn't looking, another told me my hair looked like a hack job from the 70s, and days later I received a phone call from a mother who threatened to sue me for discriminating against her son because he had a disability. Really, I don't think calling the teacher all sorts of profanity counted as Turrets, especially if that student only says such naughty things when you ask him to stop carving his name into the wall.

The first week didn't go so well. The second week was worse. Someone left a condom on the floor, two days later a student found a condom in his tuba and threatened to wrap it around someone else's neck to strangle her, and the advanced students revolted and refused to play any music because I wasn't as "cool" as the old teacher. That may have been because I enforced the school tardy policy and made them use the bathroom pass before they left the room.

I went to see the vice principal in his snug little office. Mr. Rogers was youngest VP I'd ever met, only being twenty-eight, though he was already going gray and bald. I tried to convince myself it was genetics, not the school environment.

"You're doing fine," he said. "Just remember to enforce the school rules. No cell phones allowed, give them a grade for work they turn in, and make sure you come up with an incredible selection of songs for the spring orchestra concert in May. Oh and by the way, never show any emotion. They sense weakness."

What? There was a concert? They hadn't told me that. I hoped it didn't conflict with the middle school concert I was planning. That was also scheduled for May.

By the end of the third week I wanted to quit my job. It didn't help when I bumped into Mr. Frost in the hallway outside my classroom during my ten minute prep period. And when I say bump, I mean quite literally. I was unlocking my classroom door while he stared at the ceiling, staggering and reeking of alcohol.

"Torture...scorch her...overture...pressure...oof!" That final word came out as he collided into me.

He scowled, then his expression changed to his usual aloof coolness. "Oh, it's just you. I thought you were that student trying to break in and pee in the rubbish bin again. You look like shit, by the way."

I took in a quivering breath and burst into tears.

"Oh, fuck, I hate it when the music teachers cry."

"Music teachers?" I asked.

"Yes, well, you are the sixth one in five years. It's almost like one of those Harry Potter novels with the defense against the dark arts teacher. Only I suspect you won't have the benefit of turning into a werewolf and eating students." He ripped a page from an essay he'd been carrying. "Here, use this."

I stared at the paper marked with an F+, wondering what he meant for me to do with it.

He went on, his voice dripping with exasperation. "The paper towel dispenser in your room hasn't been refilled since last year's budget cuts, and that Joshua kid with allergies probably used the last of the tissue you brought in days ago. You might as well use this as toilet paper."

I handed it back to him. "Thank you for your, uh...chivalry, but I'm fine." I wiped my face on my sleeve, feeling stupid. I'd been teaching for nine years and I was acting like I was a teacher fresh out of grad school. "I'm just not used to teaching high school," I admitted. "They're so different. You can't scare them into behaving like you can at the middle school. We don't have reward tickets here for good behavior or consequence sheets for bad behavior, the vice principal doesn't want me to use detentions unless it's for skipping, fights, or sexual harassment. And don't get me started on the bathroom pass issue." They all wanted to get out of class. I wished I could use the excuse that I had to go to the bathroom and then hide in there for the rest of the semester.

Mr. Frost wasn't even listening. He muttered under his breath, trying to rhyme words.

How stupid of me. For a moment, I had thought he might care. I turned to my classroom in disgust, unlocking the door.

Mr. Frost jerked to attention. "Just do what I do; tell them they can go to the bathroom in exchange for their immortal soul. But make sure you have them sign out in a *black* book…and it needs to be signed with their blood or else it doesn't count. It really works wonders. My students would rather break into your classroom through the utility closet we share to urinate in the rubbish bin than sign out of my class to use the bathroom. Have fun."

"Right. Thanks for the suggestion." What a creeper.

He wandered down the hallway, muttering to himself. "Blood… stud…mud…brud. Oh, fuck, that isn't even a word. I hate my life! I might as well just end it now and burn in Hell for the rest of eternity."

I'M ABOUT ready to strangle one of my students. If it hadn't been for my middle school students in the mornings and the joy on their cheery faces as I taught them Disney songs, I would have taken permanent medical leave due to stress. The vice principal was on me for giving too many detentions and of all the insults, asked me to observe Mr. Frost during my lunch break since he rarely had any discipline problems.

Considering Mr. Frost wrote an assignment on the board at the beginning of class and then sat at his desk writing his own poetry for the rest of the hour and ignored his students, I wondered what the school considered a bad teacher.

Me, apparently, or else I wouldn't be taking pointers from a lush. I picked up the black book in the corner of the classroom—his main means of classroom management. I noticed quite a few names in the book too. Most of them were written in a rust-tinted ink, the ones lower down on the list crimson.

Mr. Frost jumped out of his chair and stumbled over a stack of English textbooks on the floor to snatch the book out of my hands.

"That isn't for you," he said, replacing it on the ledge of the chalkboard. Some of the students looked up from the essay they were writing. A few of them giggled, breaking the silence of his classroom.

He glared at them. "Quiet all of you. I need silence. I'm an artist at work. After school detentions in my room to anyone who breaks my concentration."

Students exchanged apprehensive glances. A few of them stared at the leather-bound book on the chalkboard in trepidation. Was that supposed to be the difference in teaching high school versus middle school, a Machiavellian approach?

"So, are all those signatures just for leaving to use the restroom?" I asked.

His chuckle sounded especially wicked in the silence of the room. "In the beginning, yes, but now I've thought of other reasons to make them sign it. Over the years I've collected over six hundred signatures in my black book. I have less than ten to go."

"Ten until what?"

He pushed me toward the door. "Nothing. Never mind. You wouldn't understand. You aren't a poet."

Tip Number Three: Smother the little darlings with love. And when that doesn't work, use a pillow.

I was in the middle of teaching my beginning/advanced mixed

class—talk about a curriculum challenge—when Mr. Frost burst through the door, pointing a finger at me. His eyes were bloodshot. He roared over the chaotic chords of thirty students practicing their music warm ups all at different times. "You! I should never have shared my secrets with you. You're stealing souls I could be selling to Satan. Now I'll never get my soul back!"

"What?" I looked to my students who hadn't noticed the interruption in their jumble of playing. I hoped I'd misheard him.

"Don't try to deny it. Kayli Avon, the new student, asked if she could use the restroom today, and I told her she could if she signed her name in my black book. She laughed like it was a joke, and she said she had already given her soul to you in exchange for going to buy a snack from the vending machine yesterday."

I tried to keep a straight face. "Um, I'm sure there are more than enough souls to go around."

"No, there isn't! I need those souls." Blue veins bulged against his flushed skin. "The worst of it is you're such an amateur. You didn't even make her sign it in blood."

By now, some of my students had begun to notice Mr. Frost's presence. A few of them stopped playing. One of my students approached, ignoring the red-faced English teacher.

Mark Juarez thudded his saxophone on the music book on my desk. "I'm not going to play this music. It's stupid."

I had been warned about Mark's temper from the school guidance counselor; he'd been raised by two drug-addict parents who now were recovered, but felt so guilty over the past, they let him do whatever he wanted, creating a spoiled brat.

"Now isn't the time," I said through clenched teeth.

Mark dropped his sax with a thunk. "Why don't I get a solo in the concert? I'm better than Jennifer. You're just playing favorites."

Mr. Frost's face scrunched up in disgust as he looked at Mark. He shook his head at me. "I'll be merciful and take care of this for you." He rounded on Mark. "You're so pathetic, your parents probably have to pretend to like you."

Mark picked up his instrument. For a second I thought he might hit Mr. Frost. But the veteran teacher pulled a small carton of cigarettes out of his breast pocket and tossed it to Mark. The kid caught it, looking confused.

"I'll pay you in cigarettes if you promise to go home and stay there for the rest of the week."

I pried the cigarettes out of Mark's hand, shoving them back at Mr. Frost. I turned to Mark. "Go sit down and practice your warm ups. I'll talk to you when I'm done." I glared at Mr. Frost. "You can't say that to kids. You'll be fired." Plus he'd damage their fragile psyche—not something I suspected he gave a rat's ass about.

"I wish. I will always be employed in this Hell hole. That's part of the problem. It was in my contract with my master," he sighed, a low miserable moan that could have rivaled a Hollywood mummy.

"Ms. Duuuuuunn!" one of the girl's screamed. She held up her flute. Something blue was stretched over it. Oh joy. One of them had brought in condoms from the health room again.

Mr. Frost rolled his eyes. "We have things to discuss. Tell your students to go away. End class thirty minutes early today."

"I can't do that! I'll lose my job!" Besides that, there was no way I wanted to be left alone with Mr. Frost.

"Oh right, you have a normal contract. Good for you, that means you can get out before you go insane. Well, have fun. I'll be in later."

AT LAST I was alone in my classroom. I was still rattled from Mr. Frost's outburst, as well as the most recent fight that had broken out over the flute-condom incident. Things had gone downhill from there: during the last period of the day, Jamari White had threatened me for looking at him across the room and grown more disruptive from there.

Usually I went home around 3:45 p.m., the scheduled time if I didn't have too many papers to grade. But on days like this, I usually let the last period go a couple minutes early so I could rush out the door when the bell rang at 3:05 and go home and eat hot fudge out of the jar as I cried.

Wouldn't you know it, right at 3:06 p.m., just as I was about to lock up, a man strode through the door, blocking my exit to chocolate nirvana and my intended therapy.

"Tisk tisk, you aren't trying to leave work early, are you?" he asked. A wicked smile adorned his cherub-like lips. He loomed over me in the same way Josh Dormler, that intimidating football student did.

"That was a move straight out of Frost's book today, throwing Jamari's bag out in the hall when he was being disruptive and locking the classroom door behind him," he said.

Please don't be Jamari's father—or any of the other bad students' fathers. Though, there was something about the casualness of his attire: the "Hug a Tree" T-shirt; long, silver ponytail; and Buddhist prayer bead bracelet, that didn't speak of irate parent on drugs bent on telling me off for giving his son a detention.

The man stepped into the room, eying the broken pencil sharpener hanging on the wall by one hinge. One would have expected a set of Birkenstock sandals to match the hippie attire. Instead there were a set of black, polished hooves. My heart caught in my throat. I had never bought into religion. But it was hard to refute what my eyes were seeing.

He strolled past the permanently locked student cubbyholes the previous teacher had lost the key to, glanced in the garbage can that I hoped wasn't full of urine today, and stopped before the wobbly choir bleachers in the back. He opened his arms, palms up as he gazed at his surroundings with pleasure in his eyes. "Ah, one of my finer works. It really is Hell on Earth in here, isn't it?"

I considered whether he meant the asbestos falling out of the ceiling in the corner where the music stands were stored, or he meant the chaos of the classes. Unable to make my voice work, I stared at him mutely.

"I can see you're a busy woman, so I'll cut to the chase. You are making unauthorized bargaining of souls without my permission."

I turned on the lights, blinking. I tried not to stare at his feet. "Um, what?"

"The black book with the signatures." Satan seated himself at one of the uncomfortable stools in front of the student tables, grunted and smiled as if pleased at finding it so ergonomically-challenged. "Of course, only the ones signed in blood count, but you've racked up five of those so far. Not bad for your first month. Frost only got four in his first semester here."

"What? Mr. Frost gets students' souls for you?" I mean, he'd said as much, but I also thought he was the mayor of crazy town.

Satan tapped on the desk with pointed black fingernails that resembled claws. "If you join me and work as my agent, I'll fulfill your deepest wishes. You need only tell me what that wish is."

I crossed my arms. "Yeah, just like you did with Mr. Frost."

Satan shrugged, a mischievous smile tugging at his lips. "Frost is a special case. He sold his soul to me in exchange for a teaching position at this school when the economy was bad. He only gets it back when he reaches six hundred and sixty-six souls. Of course, the idiot will probably sell his soul back to me again in exchange for being able to come up with the perfect rhyme. Or maybe he'll ask for green eyes next time." He chuckled.

"So those students, the ones who signed my book, you really own their souls? But they didn't know. They thought it was a joke."

"As I said, just the ones in blood. The ones who really meant it." He shrugged, indifferently. "It's not as though you like any of the ones that are mine. Consider: Rosa Bustraun is sabotaging your upcoming class concert with all her drama. Do you really mind if I own her soul? Jennifer Little openly defies you on a daily basis, but the vice principal isn't going to do anything about it because he's sleeping with her."

My jaw dropped.

He waved me off dismissively. "Don't worry, I sooo own the VP. There's a special place in Hell for him." He laughed wickedly. "Then there's Andre Martinelli who threatened to punch you yesterday. And Jamari White, the one who has been sneaking the condoms—"

"He's the one?" I interrupted.

Satan chuckled. "Children do the darnedest things, don't they? My point is, all of those students deserve burning in Hell for all of eternity. They'll never be anything more than delinquent, Generation Me, hell-raisers who will do the world more bad than good. If it's not you who sells me their souls, Mr. Frost will. You might as well get something out of it. What is your greatest desire?"

I considered what it would be like to have complete classroom management, total control over this group of juvenile delinquents. I imagined the high school students behaving as well as my middle school students.

A smile curled to Satan's lips. I shook my head, seeing the path I was being lured down. No, I would not compromise the souls of my students for my own personal gain. Surely the road to Hell was paved with such compromises.

"You can't tempt me," I said.

"Really? Not even by making chocolate Sundays low-carb and fat-free? Not even by giving you fulltime employment at the middle school? How about by giving you an administrator with realistic expectations?"

"No." I quivered with yearning, but I forced my hands to clench into fists to hide the way they wanted to reach out and grasp any of those offers. Even so, I felt my resolve weakening. "What do you do with their souls once they've signed my book? Do you make them do anything? Like kill people? Make teachers' lives Hell on Earth."

"No, they have free will to do as they please. I just influence the world around them and wait until they die. Usually I don't have to wait long. You'll be thanking me, really."

I thought again about the five students whose souls he now owned. Five less juvenile delinquents in the world....No, I couldn't. I was a horrible person just for thinking about it.

I lifted my chin. "I think their souls are worth something. It isn't too late for them." Or for me, I silently added. I would not turn into Mr. Frost. "I want their souls back. They didn't know they were selling their souls."

Satan sighed. He turned his palms up as though he had just been defeated. "You are just too good. Has anyone ever told you that? I suppose something could be worked out. If you really think they're worth it...prove it. If you can get them to be too good for Hell, you can have their souls back, the ones in blood and any others in your book. If you can't, your soul also will be mine." Satan extended his hand toward me.

I hesitated. Was I setting myself up for failure? Still, I could not allow those students to suffer as a result of what I'd unwittingly done. I shook his hand, wincing at the prick of his claws against my flesh.

"Now if you'll excuse me," Satan said. "I need to make a guest appearance in the detention room...."

Tip Number Four: You have to stay one step ahead of them.

I peeked my head in the door to Mr. Frost's classroom. My stomach churned. I hated talking to him. But I had to get back the souls of the five students who had signed their names in blood. And he was my best hope.

He stared at the ceiling, leaning back in his chair. "Die...lie... why...nigh...high. Fucking shit."

The class of students sat reading. It was as silent as a graveyard. Even with Satan's help, I didn't see how he did it.

I approached his desk and lowered my voice to a whisper. "I just came to apologize." I hoped I looked sincere. I'd also put on lipstick. It wouldn't make me look earnest, but at least I looked attractive. It might distract him.

Mr. Frost raised an eyebrow. "I'm listening."

I glanced over the students. Was he going to make me say this publicly? "Um, I had a little visit from you-know-who. I didn't realize I was infringing on your territory."

He rose and sauntered over to the door. Glancing over his class he said, "If anyone gets up while I'm out of the room, I'm going to assign a detention. In Hell."

No one dared make a sound. He closed the door. "Have you anything else to say?"

"Besides that you're a brilliant poet? I typed your name into the internet and did a Google search. Wow, I had no idea you knew so many, um, rhymes."

He smiled at me now. "Yes, I am rather clever, aren't I?"

"Anyway, I was hoping you could help me. I don't want to be responsible for all those souls going to Hell. I wondered if you could tell me how I might be able free them—you know, so you could get them instead."

"Hmm." His icy blue eyes narrowed with suspicion. I held my breath. "Yes, I suppose I could take them off your hands. I should tell you how this works. It isn't so much about the written in blood thing—though that helps. It's really about intention. There's that saying, 'Good intentions pave the way to Hell.' But bad intentions never pave the way to heaven.

"What else…? You get bonus points for getting teachers to sign in your book. And you don't have to get them to sign it if they'll at least say it out loud. You can tempt an adult to do something illicit like get a student with mono to cough on a student's desk who you…oh."

Perhaps my glare reminded him he had tried to convince me to do that. I asked, "So you were trying to get me to sell my soul to Satan?"

"It isn't anything personal. Anyway, back to our little problem. If you can get them to change their intentions, repent, or maybe get them to do something selfless, that may free their souls. Then again, it might just be easier to throw water balloons filled with holy water at them and play gospel music in the background so they can become born-agains. Well, have fun with that."

If Mr. Frost was right, I had to get these kids to do something profoundly good. I had to show Satan their souls were worth saving. Here's what I knew about the five students whose soul's belonged to Satan:

Rosa Bustraun: drama queen and major behavior influencer on the other girls. Both parents worked for the same corporation and were rarely home.

Jennifer Little: sexually-abused by mother's former boyfriend and now sleeping with the vice principal

Andre Martinelli: regularly threatened to punch other students and adults. He had been an ideal student four years ago. His grades had gradually slipped and he became emotionally unstable when his younger sister had died of leukemia two years ago.

Jamari White: his abusive mother was currently in jail. His father and brother had died in a house fire when he was a child.

Mark Juarez: former drug addict parents and current narcissist.

All these kids, and a few others not on Satan's list, had tough childhoods and never found constructive ways to deal with loss or abuse or disappointment. They had learned it was safer not to care. Somehow, I was going to have to learn to make them care again.

IN THE darkness of the classroom, a few students whispered as the first image projected onto the screen at the front of the room, the cheery notes of Mozart's "Divertimento in D Major" playing in the background. I used the digital projector from the middle school connected to my laptop to project the Power Point slide show I'd put together with the help of my morning middle school classes.

"This is a happy, healthy five-years-old. His name: Juan Chavez." I mentioned a few other facts about his life, his favorite color, his pet's name. The music switched to the slow, sad notes of Beethoven's "Moonlight Sonata," the images of James changing to those of him in the hospital, dark circles under his eyes, his black hair disappearing as the chemo progressed. "Juan developed a rare form of leukemia. He underwent treatments for five years." The slideshow flipped through an array of photos of him growing thinner and weaker as time passed, ending with the image of his grave. "He died this year."

The students ceased talking. A few of them who'd had their headphones on now removed them. Rosa stared at the screen, tears in her eyes. For once she wasn't talking.

The next song started, an upbeat Michael Jackson song as I spoke about the next child. The screen showed a smiling little girl hugging her teddy bear. The images progressed to the house demolished by a fire, her bandaged little body in the hospital, the stumps where her fingers used to be, and angry red scars on her face. "Yesterday" played softly in the background. A sniffle came from Jamari White's area of the room.

I showed more children, victims of abuse and neglect, babies of drug-addict parents born premature.

A rough, hoarse baritone shouted over the music. "What's any of this got to do with orchestra?"

Just the opening I had been waiting for. I turned down Sarah McLaughlin's "Angel" the images continuing on. "What do you hear in the background?"

"Duh, music," one of the girls said. "Two of those songs we've been working on in class."

"So how does it make you feel?"

A few shouted out answers: sad, depressed, sleepy—that last one was from Jamari White.

"This is music theory. Music affects mood. It's used in movies, in advertising, in political campaigns. It can be used to manipulate people's feelings, and it can be used as therapy and make someone feel better. We are going to have Emmerson's Spring Concert in three months. I've already talked to the principal about making this one a charity benefit for Dornbecker's Children's Hospital. All those children you saw in the slideshow today are, or were once, patients at the hospital. Any donations we receive at the concert will go toward those children's treatments and making their lives a little better. I am going to put this class in charge of the slide show at the concert."

Students turned to each other and began to whisper. Jamari White stood and walked out of the classroom without taking the hall pass. I wondered if I might have overestimated his ability to feel sympathy.

The presentation in the other classes went well. Mark Juarez gasped when he saw the premature baby, muttering, "I was just like him when I was born."

When I turned on the lights, Andre Martinelli told the class about his younger sister who died of leukemia.

Jamari White approached me as I was locking up after school. "I've been working on a song about my brother. But I can't get all the notes right. If I bring in my guitar, could you help me write down the notes? Maybe it's something I could play at the concert."

Now awaited the true challenge. I went to Mr. Frost's room.

As usual, he stared at the ceiling, feet crossed on his desk as he leaned back in his chair. "Droll…pole…soul…."

"Um, excuse me," I said. "I wondered if I could request your expertise for the music concert I'm putting on."

He continued staring at the ceiling. "If you're going to ask whether I think you should allow the orchestra to play the Michael Jackson song they've been practicing in class, the answer is no. That's just an invitation for the boys to grab themselves in front of the entire school."

"Um, actually, that wasn't what I was going to ask. I wondered if you would be willing to share your literary talent with the school and write a poem for our event. I have a list of songs and the content of the slide shows so you can see what we're looking for."

Frost sat up in his chair. "I suppose I could grace your event with my literary genius. But don't expect those illiterate cretins to recognize true talent when they see it."

AFTER MONTHS of hard work, long hours, and countless bad dreams about going to Hell with all my students—which truly would be eternal punishment—came the long awaited evening.

The night of the concert, the school gym swarmed with the parents of the high school students as well as those of my middle school students. A combined concert. I wiped my clammy palms on my skirt and drew in a deep breath. The article printed in the local newspaper had drawn in the rest of the crowd. No big deal to stress about, right?

Maybe I should have listened to Mr. Frost about not using a Michael Jackson song. There were so many ways the students might ruin this night.

There were also many ways Mr. Frost might ruin the night, especially if he chanced to look in his black book and saw what I had done.

I paced in front of the art on the walls provided by the art teacher's classes. For the jillionth time, I checked my watch. I nodded to Rosa Bustraun at the door who ducked out to turn off the lights from the gym teacher's office. Before the room darkened, I spotted the man in the crowd with a silver ponytail and a tie-dyed shirt that said: "The children shall inherit the Earth."

I tried to swallow the lump in my throat but it remained.

The spotlights above the orchestra and middle school choir flickered on. The middle school started with a peppy tune from Mary Poppins. On the screen, images of flowers, rainbows and joyful children flashed across the screen. Quotes about the children pictured were interspersed, making the children come alive. After the first song, Andre Martinelli stepped up to the microphone, sharing an essay about his sister. The high school and middle school students took turns with their performances, slideshows projected during the pieces. After the first four songs, the photos and music grew more somber. Jamari White sang about his brother who died in the house fire as he played the guitar, his voice cracking. Twice I stepped forward, about to walk him off stage when he choked up, but each time he recovered enough to continue.

Then came my most anxious moment: Mr. Frost's poetry.

I had no idea what to expect. He'd insisted he would only write a poem if he didn't have to share it until the night of the event. For all I knew, he might focus on his pathos as an unrecognized poet. Or he might accuse me of tearing the pages out of his black book. Which would be true.

He cleared his throat at the microphone. His cold, blue eyes raked over the crowd. He placed a pair of black-rimmed spectacles on his nose. The paper crinkled in his hands. I held my breath as the first words slipped out over the sea of bodies.

"The heart of a child,
Loving and tender,
Dreams defiled,
With no defender.
The loss of innocence,
The loss of youth,
Taken without sense—"

"Ms. Dunn," a student whispered. "Jimmy just puked in Maria's tuba."

I delegated a few high school students to oversee the clean up while I listened to the rest of Mr. Frost's poem. He'd actually taken the request seriously and put heart into it. He'd written something beautiful and done something selfless for others.

The remaining half hour of the concert passed blissfully, the slide show focusing on individual success stories. Interwoven in a musical tapestry of hope, the photos showed my students at Dornbeckers Children's Hospital interacting with the young patients.

They came to the microphone and made suggestions on how the community could get involved.

We ended on the song, "The Devil Went Down to Georgia."

Even after the event was over, the crowd lingered. My colleagues congratulated me on the success of the event. Students conversed with friends, reeling over the high of doing well. The parent volunteers at the door told me we had raised over two thousand dollars in one night.

I had done it. My students had achieved something beyond what they had ever done before; they helped others and all showed they had hearts—souls unworthy of Hell. But was it enough to get those five souls back? And to keep my own?

Satan had said he would free all the souls *in my book*—which is why I had broken into Mr. Frost's room to tear out the pages of student signatures in his black book and put them in mine just before the concert. Obviously, he hadn't noticed yet.

Jennifer Little approached me, Rosa and two other girls behind her. "Ms. Dunn, that was a good turn out and all, but I don't think we did enough. I mean, don't you think it would be better to perform at Dornbeckers for the kids?"

"We wouldn't do the same slide show—we don't wanna make them sad, but we could do something else," Rosa said.

"What do you have in mind?" I asked.

The three girls looked at each other before Jennifer went on. "Rosa and I were talking about putting together a different kind of slideshow, you know, a happy one. We could play our happier songs—if you think the kids might like that."

I smiled. Tears filled my eyes. "Yes, I think they would like that."

I SLEPT in until noon the next day, a Saturday, and then went to the grocery store. If there was one thing I deserved after months of work, it was a huge ice cream Sunday.

As I passed the natural food section of the store, I blinked and did a double-take. At the end of the bulk food isle, scooping granola out of a bin, was Satan. Apparently, even the devil needed fiber.

His shirt today said, "Reduce, reuse, recycle…and listen to really good music." His black eyes met mine. "Good afternoon to you, Ms. Dunn. Splendid concert you put on the other night."

My gaze flickered to his hooves. The other woman in the aisle, a patchouli-wearing hippie in patchwork bell-bottoms didn't notice.

I swallowed my fear. "Are you here to collect my soul?"

He dragged a pointed, black nail over a silver eyebrow. "Come now, it's my job to punish evil-doers, not those beyond temptation. You proved me wrong. Those students' souls were worth saving. My ownership of all of them in your book has been dissolved." A little smile quirked the corners of his mouth upward as if sharing a joke with me. "You even did Mr. Frost a bit of good."

I waited for the 'but.' It didn't come.

"What? Did you think I'd be a sore loser?" His raised an eyebrow. "I'm not all bad, you know. I once was an angel. I'm very good at bringing out the best in people—and the worst in others. It seems I've brought out the best in you. As far as Frost is concerned, well, he brings out the worst in himself without my help." Satan picked out a nugget of granola from the bag he held and popped it in his mouth. "Mmm. Maple date, my favorite. Some things on Earth are just too good to mess with."

Tip Number Five: No matter how good of a teacher you are and how passionate you are in what you teach, it is important to remember that you can't reach every student.

When I unlocked the door Monday afternoon during my lunch/prep, Mr. Frost was already in my classroom. He sat in one of the uncomfortable student stools, his black book clenched in is hands.

"You were the one who stole my signatures, weren't you?" His eyes narrowed. There was something unsettling about his eyes—more unsettling than his usual cool gaze.

I flipped on the lights. "Satan implied he gave you your soul back. Was I mistaken?"

He lifted his chin, staring at the ceiling like a petulant child. "That isn't the point. I needed those souls. I made another bargain with him."

That's when I noticed how vividly green his eyes were.

I flopped my purse down on my desk. "Wait a minute. You didn't trade your soul just to change your eye color, did you? You have heard of color contacts, right?"

"They itch my eyes."

Obviously, I couldn't save everyone's soul. Some people brought Hell upon themselves. I shook my head. "You could have had heaven when you died, but chose green eyes."

He jumped to his feet, a hand raised melodramatically to his forehead. "This will be my Hell for all of eternity; teaching high school English when I could be the most brilliant poet who ever lived."

"Hmm, well, have fun with that," I said. I opened my grade book, ready to start another rewarding afternoon with a great group of kids.

Sarina Dorie is the author of award-winning, YA paranormal romance novel, *Silent Moon*. Her Puritan and alien love story, *Dawn of the Morning Star*, is due to come out this year with Wolfsinger Publications. She has sold over sixty short stories to markets like Daily Science Fiction, Magazine of Fantasy and Science Fiction, Orson Scott Card's IGMS, Cosmos, and Sword and Laser. By day, Sarina is a public school art teacher, artist, belly dance performer and instructor, copy editor, fashion designer, event organizer and probably a few other things. By night, she writes. As you might imagine, this leaves little time for sleep. www.sarinadorie.com

Reduce. Reuse. Recycle.

Alexis Duran

JAKE WONDERED WHY HE WAS IN THE BATHTUB with his clothes on. Icy moonlight wavered in the through the obscuring glass and stroked the ceiling with crystalline wave patterns. The faucet dripped a rhythm he couldn't quite place. His fingers curled stiff and blue against the white porcelain. He hadn't planned on dying so young, but then he hadn't planned on being a drug-addicted sex worker either.

Alternately aware and unaware of his surroundings, his skin tingled and then went numb. His heart fluttered then stalled. Droplets from imaginary steam slid down blue tiled walls and collected on his eyelashes. He tried moving, but that didn't pan out. He relived the choices that led to this moment, this pathetic death in a stranger's bathtub. He vaguely remembered collapsing into it after heaving his guts out in the toilet.

He'd chosen to accept the packet of white powder from Art, the sleaziest pusher in the zone. He'd chosen to inject the full dose, remembering that Natasha was expecting him that night. Maybe that's why the extra shot seemed like a good idea. Natasha got her money's worth, always.

He never would have chosen to die in a bathtub, yet he had chosen and he worried briefly about what Hell would be like, but then remembered he didn't believe in Hell. The tub formed a tactile, cool dimension into which he could disappear, if he chose. Or could he? He couldn't move, up or down, in or out. He was stuck. An acute fear gripped him, worse than dying or Hell; paralysis. What would they do with a quadriplegic whore? The state wouldn't support that mess for long. Shady Sadie wouldn't pay for his upkeep, that was for sure.

The rubbery arm laid out along his hip bothered him. It looked unreal. Why didn't he go under? Was there water in the tub after all? Drowning would be a mercy, not this slow slide, this awareness that he'd killed himself by accident. No one else to blame. *The druggie mother is nowhere to be seen now, Jake. You slid the needle into your own thigh.* He didn't want to spend his last moment in a pity party. He wanted to see Gigi. He wanted to say good-bye and I'm sorry. To tell her he hadn't meant to die.

He smelled bleach. Lavender oil. Natasha loved lavender. He couldn't see anymore, only sense. He sensed someone enter the room. Someone, maybe Gigi. Maybe there was time. How much time had passed? Minutes? Seconds? Maybe they could revive him. If only he could get their attention.

He heard Art's voice reverberate against the tiles,

"Some take longer to die than others."

IF NATASHA had any qualms about recycling Jake's body, she got over them when Steve 1 arrived. She had worried about, well, about decay, but obviously the company had been true to their word, and the temporary loss of animation had not hurt the appearance of the flesh at all.

Steve 1 was gorgeous, of course, and on closer inspection, felt quite nice, not like previous incarnations of the New Skin robotic line. With added enhancement, like increased muscle tone and chemical purging, he appeared healthier and stronger than Jake ever had. But he still had the spun gold hair, the dark almond eyes, and most importantly, the tight tan skin that made her mouth water. Slightly feminine, but slinky sexy in a way that promised hidden strength. She had of course been saddened by news of Jake's death, but quickly jumped at the opportunity to save what she'd always loved about him most—his body.

Jake, a registered drug addict, was not an acceptable organ donor, so it had been a bit dicey, with bribes to pay and hoops to jump through, but if she was going to have a recycled robot sex toy, she wanted what she wanted. And she could pay. Jake was beyond caring, though she suspected he'd be pissed if he knew. But he didn't, and he hadn't left a will and there were no relatives to claim the remains.

It would have been a waste to send such a body to the incinerator. She'd expected Steve 1 to be more robotic, less life like, but the only thing that gave away his computer chip soul were the eyes. They were flat, shiny marbles, with none of Jake's mischievous spark to be found. They swam with the same liquid crystals as her 3-D video screen, but they were windows to nowhere.

Oh well, Steve 1's compliance more than made up for it. He was all hers. Not only did she have incredible sex at the click of a button, but he helped out with other things too. He was a walking computer after all. He could move furniture or figure her taxes, if she needed such things. She might be able to fire her human assistants, but she decided to hold off on that, to put Steve 1 through his paces first.

He wasn't much of a conversationalist. He responded, but did not initiate.

"So, Steve, what would you like your new name to be?" she asked the morning after their first long night together.

"What's wrong with Steve?" he asked, in the flat tone that took some getting used to. He stood looking out the window, or pointing his eyes out the window, which was his default setting when not servicing her needs or tending to some task.

She was about to say, use your imagination, but he didn't have one. The limitations were many, but Steve 1 was the most advanced robot yet, a melding of computer chip mind with biological neurons and pathways. A real miracle of science, and she was happy to have one of the first models available to civilians.

"Steve doesn't suit you," she said, admiring his profile. She missed Jake's quick wit and wicked smile, their teasing banter, but she didn't miss his addiction or his resistance to her quirkier desires. Steve offered no resistance. She wondered if he could be programmed to pretend to resist. Just a little. Like a volume button, she could dial up his personality when needed. That had been one of Jake's biggest drawbacks, too much personality.

"Liam," she said, thinking of her boyfriend in college, the one who'd encouraged her dominatrix leanings.

"Okay," he said.

"Or maybe Ivan. I always thought Jake looked like he might have a little Russian blood in him."

"Jake," he said. "I like Jake."

"No you don't," she said quickly. "That name has been used up. How about Gregori?"

"Okay." He looked at her, blinking infrequently. He always looked at her when she spoke to him. Another plus. Not with longing or lust, but not with contempt either.

JAKE WOKE up. Or tried to. He was having that nightmare where he knew he was asleep, that someone was in the room with him, but he couldn't move, not the way he wanted to, anyway. Instead of lying down, he stood and stared out a window. After a long struggle to turn around and see who was behind him, he subsided back into sleep. He dreamt of servicing Natasha. She was angry with him.

NATASHA WANTED to see Steve squirm. Yes, he'd been programmed to perform and respond appropriately, but sometimes appropriate didn't cut the mustard. Polite acquiescence contributed little to her passion. He responded to pain, but did he feel it? He wasn't much of an actor. Because he was a prototype, she might be able to get him rewired. She watched his back as she spoke with the geeks at New Skin, asking if she could bring him in for a tune-up.

THIS TIME Jake really woke up. Someone was doing something to him, and it hurt. Still, he couldn't move. His body felt like a suit of armor, much too heavy for his feeble energy to budge. He suspected he hadn't died after all, but he wasn't alive either. He wasn't in a hospital. Briefly, he thought he was in some kind of lab. Then back again, to the cool rooms, the wall of glass, the large bed. This then, was hell.

NATASHA SAT in her lounge, dreaming up new things to do to Steve 1. In the end, the name had stuck. It suited him after all. The tune-up had increased the range of his fake emotions, but he was no Jake. Oddly enough, as her disappointment grew, so did her excitement. She enjoyed tormenting the robotic Steve on an entirely different level, calling on her long underused imagination to fill in the emotional blanks. He reacted to pain, but the difference between pain and suffering became clear to her now. She'd started bringing in human whores again. Those who'd known Jake nearly fainted with shock. This gave her some satisfaction.

She turned off her S & M App and went to find Steve 1. She'd asked to have an intercom installed in his head, but the geeks at New Skin said there were too many appliances in there already. The wiring could overload the delicate neural network.

She walked into her cream-colored bedroom and found him, not standing by the window in his default position, but sitting at her desk. This irked her slightly. She hadn't told him to balance her bank account. She walked up behind him and glanced at the screen. The blood drained from her face. The program wasn't her financial folder but her mail. There was a message open addressed to Jake, from someone named Gigi. "Are you alive?" was all it said.

Natasha grabbed his shoulder and turned him in the chair. His beautiful face remained impassive, as always, unless she ordered otherwise. His hands were on his thighs. The message had not been answered, only opened. He must have recognized the name Jake. She slipped often enough and called him that. Maybe he'd responded to the ping. Maybe he thought she'd called him via the computer. Maybe. She deleted the message and quickly placed another product call to New Skin.

NATASHA SAT in the neutral-toned office across from the head geek of New Skin. The room was designed to be professional, objective, fully removed from the messy business of rewiring corpses.

"The human mind is an amazing organ," Dr. Bob Bridge said. Unlike his office, the doctor was messy, with uncombed hair and three-day stubble on his weak chin.

"You assured me Jake would be dead." She glared at him, completely rigid though her insides tumbled.

"He is. He was." Dr. Bridge tried to hide his excitement, but couldn't stop fingering the keyboard in front of him. "The brain has the ability to rebuild its neural pathways. We've seen this happen with victims of severe stroke. Memories once thought lost forever are actually stored deep within the ganglion tissues." He coughed and tapped the board with his thick fingers. "We've never seen this happen after death, however. And I assure you, Jake was completely dead when the medical examiner released his body to us."

"Oh, lovely." Natasha angrily flexed and straightened her fingers. "Even in death he defies me."

"I wouldn't take it personally. The impulse to survive is quite primal. To regenerate…it's really quite astounding. The affect on the world of brain research will be staggering."

"Wait just a minute." She leaned forward, hands gripping the arm of the chair. "That body belongs to me. I paid for it. Without me, it would be nothing but ash by now."

Doctor Bridge appeared startled, as if the thought she might fight to retain her property had never occurred to him. Natasha felt sweaty as thoughts and emotions clashed.

"How much of Jake actually exists?" she asked.

"Well, that's just it. We have no idea. The tests we've run show responses outside the parameters of his, of Steve 1's, programming. The electrical impulses in his brain react differently to stimuli drawn from Jake's past. The name Gigi, for instance—"

"Tell me," Natasha interrupted, "Doesn't one cease to be an individual upon death? A corpse has no rights, no legal protections. That's why recycling is possible. If you make this glitch public, your business here could very well be made illegal."

The doctor's finger tapping slowed. He scowled.

"All I want to know," Natasha continued, "is how does this affect our contract? Will I get a full refund?"

The doctor's scowl deepened. "The implications to medical science are quite profound," he said, but with less conviction. Natasha sensed that a bigger bribe might help him let go of the dreams of scientific discovery.

"I don't want to sue. I've been happy with Steve 1. He's by no means the perfect robot, but I understand the research, your research, is in the early stages. It would be a shame to jeopardize all that you've invested in New Skin."

"Yes, it would, wouldn't it?" he said. "And, these preliminary tests might be in error."

"Perhaps you should run them again, with a more objective frame of mind." She leaned back. Her heart was still pounding, but she felt she stepped back from the precipice of losing Jake forever.

JAKE KNEW he wasn't dead. Or asleep. He was definitely trapped in some kind of nightmare, though. At first he thought he'd had a stroke, or brain damage due to the overdose. But his body seemed to go on without him. He couldn't get it going, or stop it once in motion. Natasha seemed to be in charge. She'd always liked it that way.

She'd always pushed his tolerance levels for the rough stuff. Now she did what she wanted.

In a certain way he felt glad to be buried so deeply beneath his own skin. On the other hand, the more aware he became, the more urgently he wanted to escape. But no connection remained between his mind and his body. This seemed to be the source of Natasha's anger. He didn't understand her words, but his body did. His will to find the surface of his skin dimmed, and her interest in him waned.

A bell rang. Jake noticed his body moving through the white planes and beige angles. Natasha's apartment. A series of large and small boxes. His world. His Hell. His hand pushed the button that opened the threshold. His eyes saw a woman. Short. Long brown hair. Voluptuous. Painted. A whore. The words flooded his pinhole existence, slightly expanding its edges. A name, Gigi. The woman enclosed him in an embrace. Warmth seeped down from his skin. The name tried to swim to his tongue and failed. Then the lights in the hallway went out.

MORE BRIBES. More threats. More coercing. The whore named Gigi threw a fit at the sight of Steve 1, but Natasha had convinced her with reasoning and cash that Jake no longer existed. He didn't, after all, respond to her in any way. Like any woman, Gigi would rather have him dead than disinterested.

"You're a sick woman," the whore had said on her way out, with that look of contempt Natasha knew so well. But as she closed the door, she didn't feel sick. She felt quite pleased with herself and with Steve 1.

"Jake? I know you're in there Jake."

If he heard her, there was no indication of it. The eyes remained flat and cold. It had become her most ardent desire to see the flicker of life within them once more. Finally, their desires meshed.

THE WORDS trickled down.

Jake's eyes were pointed at her. They were always pointed at her. This time though, he really saw her, beyond the skin and down into her hollow soul.

She saw him, and smiled.

"I'm not a monster, Jake," she said. "Of course I'll let them help you. It's your choice. All you have to do is ask."

Alexis Duran was born and raised in the Pacific Northwest. In college, her fascination with people and relationships led her to major in Sociology, but her main love has always been creative writing. She's worked in museums, fashion, finance and film production. Her favorite job so far has been writing blurbs for old TV shows. She's had several short stories published in the mystery, horror and literary genres and is the author of the *Masters and Mages* erotic fantasy series. Her main passions besides writing are travel, photography and practical magic. She is currently working on the next *Masters and Mages* novel and several other erotic novellas. Find out more about Alexis and her published works at www.alexisduranblog.com.

Eileen and the Rock

Lisa Alber

SOME OF THE LADS STILL INSIST the stranger caused the Cashel family troubles. With all gathered around to toast old man Cashel's demise and no one the wiser, up this stranger stepped to our host, the new laird of the manor, with a *Hello brother, I'm here to claim my place*. Could have been asking for a pint for all the fanfare he spoke, and for all the quiet that spread about the drawing room you'd have thought folks were witnessing the return of the original prodigal son. The hush lasted long enough that all jumped when that vixen Eileen gave a keening wail and flopped to the floor like a rag-stuffed doll.

Down at The Deaf Justice Pub where Alan, now all of 80, still pours a Guinness the likes of none, there's others who blame the American lass, Eileen, for the family troubles. She a Boston Brahmin, lineage of Butler descent off the Mayflower so she liked to claim, but that was for shite. She was Southie Boston all the way and just the woman to bring down a solid local family.

Or, you could blame the *Birth Registry of 1930*, but that's asking for a kick in the balls around here, that registry being a most fascinating bit of local history. A matter of pride, that's right, and you'll not be blaming a piece of moldering paper for some people's peculiar obsessions.

* * *

EILEEN, NOW she was a pretty sort of girl, and on the day of old man Cashel's burial back in 1973, she sat demure as a buttercup amongst stinging nettles. She wore a clingy dress with a plunging V-neck, dark as night but hatched through with lighter strands to enhance her eyes, if you believe what Alan had to say about her. The rest of the locals merely thought as she looked soulful and innocent with her wide blue eyes and comely freckled chest. Her fiancé, Evan Cashel, wore the mandated black and cleared his throat every now and then to prove he struggled against tears, though some couldn't help noticing that his gaze rarely roamed far from Eileen's peeping cleavage.

This was the season of the flowering laburnum, whose yellow blooms scented the air sweet as harem baths while starlings busied themselves building nests in the chapel's eaves. Eileen, dear girl, missed the beauty of the day, not to mention Father O'Toole's eulogy, because her thoughts tended to gravitate to her two-carat diamond, which was bigger than those of the posh ladies on Beacon Hill, and surely her highness Mrs. Benedict would faint to see her maid's daughter now.

From pleasant fantasies of showing-up Mrs. Benedict, Eileen's reveries returned as usual to the Rock of Cashel, where the pagan kings of Munster ruled and archbishops later prayed. Up there atop the hill overlooking the village, you've seen them, the ruins of the medieval cathedral and round tower. Quite the cachet to be buried there, so that Eileen in her wraparound dresses liked to say, and now that the old man was dead—God rest his soul—she was as good as in. She imagined resting in an open casket—mahogany no less—with her face made up to perfection and a tearful procession winding up to the Rock. She'd not be lumped in with the rest of her Southie family, just another O'Leary brat with no future for her but to follow her mother into the servants' entrances of those Beacon Hill mansions and then at the end of a toiling life only have money enough for—heaven help her—cremation. Burnt to a crisp wasn't her way. She desired immortality by way of the ultimate burial plot.

By now, you're wondering how mere dirt could hold such *cachet*, as it were. This is where the *Burial Registry of 1930* enters the tale. In that fateful year the grounds around the old cathedral were closed to further burials except for certain local and living families of the time, which is to say the O'Tooles and the Shaunessys; the Finns and the McNamaras; not to mention the oldest clan of all, the Cashels. The precious dirt allotments passed on to the next generation if unused, and as old man Cashel preferred to be buried alongside his drinking mates, the rights to burial passed over the old man's son, who died of the drink at too young an age, and on to his grandson Evan. Theirs was the last unused spot up at the Rock, which, of course, added to its *cachet*.

Old man Cashel was a tugboat of a man, wide as he was tall, always fat truth be told, and those kind purveyors of dirt back in 1930 were smart enough to predict he'd grow nothing but bigger as time passed. You might be saying that it was the old man's morbid obesity that caught Evan his fair Eileen. Canny, she was, and in the way of women who instantly size up dresses on hangers, she knew there'd be space enough to fit herself in beside Evan up at the Rock. That girl set herself upon Evan, and the poor bloody sod with a wart for a brain knew nothing but bliss at her hands—literally, for she was demure by appearance only.

THERE'S SOME that claim they noticed the stranger in their midst the day of old man Cashel's funeral, but could be the whiskey talking for all that, Alan having held a pre-funereal wake at the pub for those as considered the old man their mate in the pints. Truth was, there *was* a stranger yonder by baby Finn's grave marker, standing still as a sentinel next to the limestone angel. Irish, to be sure, but not local. Not an O'Toole or a Shaunessy, not a Finn or a McNamara. He wore his hat the proper way of the Dubliner and leaned against the angel with the nonchalance of, God help us all, a Prod.

Eileen, that minx, noticed him straight away and imagined lashing him up to the canopied bed soon to reside in her private bedroom suite. Looked to be packing a sporting rod in his trousers, so she observed, and looked to be a working man at that. She sniffed with remorse that brought on sympathy from more than one spectator, all the while her thinking she'd be hard-pressed to rid herself of her old desires: those wild Southie lads with their roughened hands and untidy manners. She clenched her thighs together rather than feel them quiver at the thought of well-worked muscles on lean bodies, none of these cream-fatted hairless expanses as sported by her dear Evan.

So it was that during old man Cashel's internment, pretty Eileen fantasized her way through the eulogy and managed to endear herself to everyone all the more for her chastely pressed legs. Afterwards, Evan with his Eileen led the mourning procession along narrow lanes to the family manor. Evan, for his part, found death tedious business, but with Eileen on his arm he strolled along willingly enough, nodding at the passing comment made by his beloved about their wedding colors, cerise and silver.

"It will be lovely," said she, "yet original. We'll find the perfect altar cloth, which will be neither too ostentatious nor too modest. Speaking of which, I was thinking of the McNamara's plot up at the Rock. I took a turn the other day, you know, mourning our poor grandfather, and I walked past the McNamara's spot without remarking it."

"Hmm?"

Evan wondered if the cook had fixed up his favorite chops with mint. Surely she'd know to prepare the meal the same as any Wednesday despite the guests and the buffet table. There'd be nothing but bits and pieces for nibbling otherwise, which never suited him.

"And it seemed to me," said Eileen with the special voice she kept for Evan. She practiced an hour each day in the privacy of her boudoir: a sing-song cadence low and sweet as a lullaby, void of pretense, filled with promised pleasures, all sure to mesmerize Evan to her way of thinking. "It seemed to me," said she, "shocking that such a prominent family has no memorial stone to speak of. Why, they're as important to local history as anyone!"

"Right," Evan said and pressed a hand against his grumbling stomach.

"Oh I agree, it's not right, and I can't help but feel sad that our poor grandfather has nothing for himself there either."

"Hmm?"

"Such an astute man, you get my meaning exactly. We'll need to commission a sculpture for his spot even if he's not buried there. Why, the site itself is a national treasure. How could the Cashel family not have their own monument? I've designed it in my head already. *Cashel* across the top with the doves he loved to shoot all around the name. Everyone knows what a good shot he was in his day."

"Sounds grand," Evan said.

"Oh I agree. And how grand that we came up with the idea!"

"Spot on," he said and squeezed her arm, thinking her too perfect to know his mind before he did.

As they walked on, his thoughts returned to food and hers to the intricacies of memorial marker design. She pictured a tall monument with plenty of space on the lower majority to fit Evan's name and her own, plus modest but charming blessings perfect for tourist rubbings. Her name would then live on through the tour guides' fond stories. She sighed and leaned against Evan's arm, and the rest of the mourners thought how touching it was that she felt the emotion of the day so keenly.

All, that is, except the stranger. He kept to himself quiet as a nun's bed until an hour later when confronted with 20-foot ceilings, Irish oak banisters, mullioned windows, and gold-leafing throughout. "So this is the family seat," he said, and Alan, who was there of course, still claims he noticed a tone to the stranger's voice, a curiosity with too much pride of place to be appropriate.

Now skip forward to the aforementioned hushed moment within the manor's drawing room. Eileen, for all her sham, fainted honestly enough to hear of a new Cashel brother. No one knew what to do, caught as they were between helping her and rushing the stranger, who announced his name was Gabriel, rightful heir to the seat.

"Hold now," Evan said, "I'm thinking."

As said earlier: a wart for a brain, poor sod. While Evan pulled on his lower lip, the fair Eileen's eyelids fluttered. She flipped a hand to be sure of the diamond, remembered the birth registry, and pushed herself to her feet with the fluid movement of a woman with an agenda. She slipped in next to Evan and fashioned herself a winsome smile. "I'm sorry, you are?"

"As I said, Gabriel."

"I'm sure we can straighten out this misunderstanding. Meanwhile, please enjoy yourself for as long as you like."

Now Gabriel, he was no fool. In an instant he knew Eileen for one step above the shady ladies who took him in after he fled the nuns. Those good whores were the ones who recognized his genteel bloodlines. They insisted he seek out his birthright, that they did, and they taught him the finer points of self-preservation, not to mention a certain kind of scrappiness. Gabriel, he wasn't a bad man, only one who had long ago wearied of the gritty side of life, especially after so many years spent tracking down his family (and a fine tale this is for the future telling).

"On second thought," Eileen continued with a wrinkle to her nose, "perhaps you'd like a shower before joining us?"

"Excuse me," Evan said, listening to his grumbling insides instead of his sweetheart. "I'll check on my meal." The truth was, he couldn't think on an empty stomach, not that food improved his processing, but never you mind: he was the kindliest man you'd ever want to meet.

Meanwhile, in response to Eileen's jibe, Gabriel wandered through the mob that stood transfixed stupid as puppets on strings. *What could the man be about?* had to be going through a fair number of minds by then because Gabriel sauntered clear over to the other side of the room. That stately manor house—now part of the Irish national heritage and open to the public—sported an Italian marble fireplace big enough to spit a sheep. Gabriel parked himself behind one of the armchairs in front of said fireplace and arranged himself in a pose that looked to be straight out of a magazine for staid country living, with one ankle crossed in front of the other, hand in pocket and jacket slung behind his hip. A cocky kind of pose with his chin straight to the horizon.

"What the hell?" Alan muttered, and his wife—God bless her soul—hushed him sure enough, busy as she was memorizing details for the pub gossips.

If pretty Eileen still ogled Gabriel's rod there's no way of knowing because just that moment a crash of Wedgwood China sounded from the back of the room, and Evan was heard to yell, "Christ almighty, will you look at that?"

What, what? came the chorus except for Eileen who caught on quick enough when she spied Evan's darting glances between Gabriel and the wall above the carved mantel. "You're the bloody image of him," Evan yelled. "Brother!"

Indeed! There stood Gabriel in mimic of a portrait, circa 1920, of right honorable old man Cashel in the prime of life with jodhpurs and riding boots, ankles crossed just so, arm cocked, profile jutting. Despite the watch fob, high-starched collar, and handlebar moustache, you'd not be mistaking Gabriel for any but the old man's grandson. Some remarked later that the resemblance wasn't obvious at first because Gabriel was thin to the old man's fat but that the muttonchop sideburns turned the corner for them, this being the 1970s and Gabriel coming direct from Dublin, height of fashion he was by their parochial reckoning. Thick facial fur identical to the old man, no one could deny it, not even fair Eileen, who stood with her mouth agape before recollecting herself.

"Evan, darling," said she, "I'm still feeling faint. Could you fetch me water, please?"

"Of course."

Gabriel cast an eyebrow in his newfound brother's direction but said nothing. He wasn't likely to at that point because he knew the lay of the land. Eileen, so he'd heard, enjoyed her way well enough, and her way was mistress of the manor with its all-important Rock of Cashel perk. Despite his bloodline, Gabriel knew himself to be on shaky ground. For a moment, he wondered whether to follow his brother or stay with the fiancée. Quick-witted devil that he was—the social calculation made in the blink of an eye—he said with purpose, "You stay with your pretty wife, Brother, while I bring the water."

Despite herself, Eileen felt a blush rise. *Wife*. That most perfect of words. Gabriel knew what she was thinking even as Eileen caught herself and aimed a suspicious glance at him. More than suspicious, hers was an eyeful of glint sharp enough to scare a lesser man than Gabriel. Meanwhile, poor Evan beckoned the maid to never mind the pork chop mess on the floor and run fetch another helping.

By the time Gabriel returned with the water, the family solicitor, a Shaunessy, huddled with Evan off in a corner. He'd pulled a mass of papers from his briefcase, and those who had a mind to perused hunting scenes along the walls near enough to eavesdrop on their conversation. Later, all at The Deaf Justice agreed that unlike logic might dictate, Evan begged the solicitor to find a loophole for Gabriel. Alan still insists he heard the word *loophole* followed by Shaunessy's response that he happened to carry just such a document. And Christ, but for the first time in his simple life Evan felt decisive and certain. Poor Evan had never liked being an only child, and on this day he almost cheered down the stone walls he was that joyful to have a brother, an older one at that, and a man of such obvious intellect to oversee the wretched financials that came along with the Cashel name.

Eileen watched her beloved with rising fear. She felt Evan's energy buoyant as a puppy and knew her place up at the Rock as good as gone to Gabriel if she couldn't guide her dim-witted love along the only correct path to their shared happiness. Gabriel must go. Nothing but a bastard son, after all. Why, his mother could be anyone.

"Your water?" Gabriel said then, and was that a knowing slight of eye in her direction? "Ay-well," he continued while Eileen tried not to mind his working-man's hands and the way their palms cupped the glass. "I was that sad to learn both my mother and father are beneath the ground—but finding a brother is the saving grace."

"You have the same mother too?" said she. "I find that hard to believe."

"What can I say but that unwed pregnancy was as taboo for a couple in love as not. They were too young to marry, so off I went to the nuns, all very hush-hush of course. I'm this glad my parents married in the end. Seems they even came to fetch me, but by then I was long gone."

Eileen felt faint. Gabriel, the heir apparent. Not some bastard, but a full brother to her Evan, who was just then waving a codicil like he'd won the bloody pot of gold. "Holy hell, it's all here left in my own grandfather's writing!"

There's some who swear Eileen lost her polish then. Was that a most unbecoming curl of lip? The beginning of a snarl low in her throat? Alan swears it's so and that he began to wonder about the fair Eileen the moment she grabbed the handwritten addendum from the solicitor Shaunessy with not a *please* or a *thank you*, not even a simper or a coy blink.

While Evan pulled Gabriel into a hug to embarrass the good Father O'Toole, Eileen read the following words and profound words they were:

As my son went the way of the dodo before me, I add this adden-

dum to my last will and testament that his dying wish be granted. Namely, that if his oldest son who was left to the nuns with the name Gabriel ever be found, he be considered patriarch after me with the responsibilities and rewards this entails, which shall include ownership of Cashel Manor and lands, hostelries along the west coast and other business ventures, and burial rights at the Rock of Cashel. (At this, Eileen blanched white as curdled milk.) *Evan as second son shall always have rights to life in the manor, a generous living, and an appropriate position within the family businesses.*

You could have thrown out the whiskey and still called the wake brilliant the surprise that spread through the room. Old man Cashel, fair-minded and generous indeed! And no one was happier than wart-for-brain Evan who fairly skipped around the parlor calling out for champagne.

This could be a corseted story written by that randy bastard Oscar Wilde the way the entailment went down, yet so it was that even in post-war, post-independent Ireland the Cashels maintained the tradition of oldest son as heir. And dearest Eileen with no say in the matter, poor thing.

She let Evan's unseemly joy peter out on its own—it wouldn't do to appear churlish after all—and when he finally stood over the back of an armchair panting for a refill of chops with mint, she tucked an arm around his elbow and whispered into his ear.

Around the couple, guests toasted Gabriel, and Alan himself pulled out a fiddle. Gabriel let himself be feted while keeping gimlet glance on his almost sister-in-law. You might be asking what he thought of her now that he knew his position solid within the family. Why, he shouldn't have minded her influence over Evan now, perhaps even have looked on their relationship with amused condescension, he having long ago lost all romantic notions about the fairer sex.

Alas and however, he did mind her influence, her wiles, her provocative chest heaves, and most of all, her continued presence in his new home. He'd lived with enough tarts in his gritty days, and he could stomach no more. Simply put, he considered himself a lifelong bachelor with no needs except shagging on the sly. That he'd already pondered buxom Eileen for such a tumble goes without saying—a tart was a tart, after all—but to live with her? Now there was a potential hell worse than the nuns ever lashed into him.

While Gabriel sipped champagne and imagined a ride on the fair Eileen before tossing her to the glue farm called the curb, that Eileen, she continued whispering into her beloved's ear.

"Oh, I agree, it's wonderful," said she, "but our grandfather forgot to be fair."

The chops with mint arrived and Evan tucked in with the alacrity of the starved. You'd have thought he'd gone without when in fact the remains of the first chop glistened on his chin. "Hmm?" he said. "I don't follow."

"You're just humoring me now, you wretch," said she and reminded herself to put the lullaby into her voice despite her frayed nerves. "You darling wretch of a man, I know you get my meaning that something's owed you for seeing grandfather through his illness."

"Well," Evan said.

"*Well* is right," said she. "It's your deep well of filial duty that saw his last days peaceful." She resisted the urge to wipe meat juice off her darling's face and continued, "Why even a token to show his gratitude."

"Token?"

"Like the tokens of love you give me each day," said she, all the while aiming her glint at Gabriel, who raised his glass toward her with a wink—how dare he? What could the horrid man possibly mean by that? Though deep down she knew his thoughts well enough, and indeed she did, for Gabriel had just then decided that the sooner he cut Evan's cord to her joyful mound, the better for them all. Fair Eileen who knew the value of the female genitalia battled her vocal cords to remain sonorous into her beloved's ear even as she absorbed—and enjoyed, don't you be doubting it—Gabriel's lingering stare at her breasts. Outrageous man.

"A token, that's all," said she. "No need to be greedy, after all. You and I, we have simple needs. A roof over our heads."

"Which we still have," Evan said, complacent with pork and unheeding of the gristle stuck between his teeth.

"Indeed," said she, "and we're the lucky ones. We have all we need to enjoy our living days." She heaved a breath as much in disgust at her beloved's continued cow-like chewing as to cause her pert breasts to inflate against his arm. "But I fear for our dying days."

Evan grunted a question mark.

"Gabriel doesn't care about the Rock surely," said she. "Not like you do, and besides, the two of you will never fit side by side in the plot. Our grandfather surely meant to leave his burial spot to you as his token."

"Ah right, the token."

His tone remained puzzled and Eileen pushed her breasts more firmly against his arm. "You see my meaning as usual—how I love you. You and I shall nestle side by side into eternity with the tour guides to tell our love story. Why, our grandfather said so on his last day, you know, he was that fond of me. Poor man, he was too sick to change his will."

"Too sick, indeed he was." Evan slurped on bone strong enough to suction out the marrow. A minute later he said, "Oh, I follow."

"Of course you do," said she. "No doubt Gabriel will heed our grandfather's intent even if it's not in writing. At least I hope so."

"Well, why not? He seems a jolly sort, but."

Hello, what was this? A *but* coming just as she felt relief like the last breath before sleep? Never had Evan *but*ted his dear Eileen, never had he seen fit to muster an independent thought while she whispered in his ear. Her previous fear turned to desperation at this oddity, and she blamed the interloper Gabriel who now tossed back a jig of whiskey and made merry with *her* locals. Look at him carrying on with them, quite in league as it were, and why should she be surprised what with his working-man's hands and atrocious manners to go along with his too-tight trousers. Imagine, introducing himself at Grandfather's wake. How gauche.

While Eileen's thoughts ran amuck, Evan considered the state of his stomach and decided another helping of chops with mint would not be amiss, this being a celebration and all.

HOLD NOW, here's a pause required because Alan always calls attention to this turning point for the family Cashel. Most of the lads argue against him, but Alan works with a few brain cells even now and 'tis true that this was the moment of reckoning. Nothing momentous, mind you, just bits and pieces that went missing or astray, that if not, could have seen the family fertile to this day.

What went missing was a thought or two on Eileen's part. She that was canny got so lost in growing anger (self-righteous at that) that she missed the chance to hear her beloved out. Instead, she took that lingering *but* as a personal affront and huffed to the closest bathroom to throw a silent tantrum.

As for the wart-for-brain, if not for his cravings, he'd have finished the thought: *but I wouldn't want to hurt Gabriel's feelings.* Meaning he was on task to ask fair Eileen's advice on how best to approach his new brother about relinquishing the burial rights. Evan's thoughts strayed often enough, too true, but sometimes they returned. Only now, with his fiancée not there to help him along, all was lost.

If only fair Eileen had heard her beloved through and if only Evan had thereafter broached the topic with Gabriel, why it's some that say Gabriel might have turned his attitude around. They'd be calling correct on that score because the moment Evan called for yet more chop with mint, Gabriel felt within himself a welling solicitude toward his younger brother, a paternalism that took him by surprise.

Look at the wanker with drippings on his tie: he deserved his happiness. Gabriel cared nothing for a patch of soil within a tourist attraction, and witnessing the weepy love in Evan's eyes for his Eileen nearly thawed Gabriel's heart enough to allow her respite—though in the opposite wing as he, of course.

Alas, the potential melt iced over again when Gabriel observed Eileen's parting shot of anger, not to mention disgust, aimed at her beloved. He grinned to himself as he threw back another shot. Got you now, he thought.

THERE'S NOTHING so grim as a woman who dares not scream, and Eileen in the bathroom was a sight to cause nightmares. She stomped back and forth on the area rug with fists waving in the air and mouth yawning open like that famous painting. Her neck tendons stood in relief and sweat (yes!) glistened on her brow, and when she finished, she stood heaving those lovely breasts in true agitation. For several minutes, she concentrated on her diamond. She let its refracting wink calm her back to her Southie street-wise roots.

Why, the solution was obvious, that classic female strategy: nothing more than good-night kisses for Evan until he saw the error of his *but*.

Back in the parlor with the festivities reaching a pitch to shatter glass, Gabriel lounged with his brother. They made quite the picture, Gabriel and Evan, sitting with knees spread and whiskeys in hand, both with the sturdy Cashel jaw, the one firm, the other slack, but the same nonetheless.

"What say you?" Gabriel said. "I take it we're square?"

"You're feckin' straight we're square. This is the best feckin' day of my life!"

"Good, good."

"Only Eileen seems a bit put out, she does." Evan shrugged. "Must be the stress of the day. She'll be fine given a moment."

Gabriel had his doubts, which were confirmed two seconds later when Eileen regained the room. She flashed a smile at Alan that further gathered the tension around her jaw. "Play on," she called with a tad too much shrill for anyone's liking.

Gabriel noted the red leaking from her cheeks when she caught sight of them cozy on the couch, which was a tableau he had orchestrated especially for her. That scrappiest of fellas had also called for yet another chop with mint so now Evan sat there with yet more dribblings on his face and tie, and his suit jacket open to reveal straining trousers—and not in the arousing way as Eileen was sure to observe. In short, Gabriel read dearest Eileen's switch of allegiance clear as if she'd straddled him with her wraparound dress hiked to the heavens.

MARK THIS as the truth: For fair Eileen, it wasn't much of a jump from withholding sex to tossing Evan away all together. Where everyone else in the room remarked on the brothers' similarities, Eileen—she that was fastidious and dainty—convulsed at their differences. Why, that must be her beloved's, rather *ex*-beloved's, fourth chop with mint, and he with his greasy face and his suit all but ruined and his slack stomach near to popping off his trouser button. Clear as the best Guinness is dark, Eileen realized there would be no controlling Evan. The wart was doomed to follow in his grandfather's obese footsteps. By the time they reached old age she'd be squeezed out of her place up at the Rock by 150 pounds of excess lard.

Gabriel, on the other hand, lounged weedy as a hawthorn branch. She sized him up and found him the better for his boniness. Even allowing for an extra 20 or 30 pounds, there'd still be space enough for her up at the Rock. In her imagination *Evan* disappeared off the monument marker to be replaced by *Gabriel*. Yes, Gabriel, who sat as lean and tidy as a dandy of old, clearly the master of his impulses, whether keeping them in line (food) or giving way to them (sex). She shivered, and it was this tremble that Gabriel caught from across the room. He kept his smile to himself, that he did, and right into his trap that Eileen came with hips a-sway and lips a-shine to settle herself between the brothers Cashel on the couch.

"My two favorite men," said she. Her hand brushed Gabriel's thigh before settling on her own. The way he then positioned his bulge in her direction, why, she as good as had him seduced with Evan none the wiser. If Mrs. Benedict on Beacon Hill could see her now, the most popular girl to rival Scarlett O'Hara!

"Grand, grand," Evan mumbled between chews. "I knew you'd come around. Lovely, really. And Gabriel here just agreed to walk you down the aisle."

Gabriel tickled her ear with his breath. "With my heartiest congratulations."

He cradled her hand in both of his and lifted it to his lips so slowly dear Eileen felt the melting between her thighs.

"Evan, darling," said she, "you might want to change now that you've got half a pig down your front."

She noticed neither the greasy kiss that landed on her cheek nor his response—*so good of you to notice; I'll do just that*—as her every sense converged on the press of her you-know-whats against Gabriel, who shifted closer with arm snaked along the couch cushion behind her.

"I must apologize for my earlier behavior," he said. "Defensive, I suppose, that ready to be tossed out on me arse."

His candor charmed her as did the way his fingers teased the back of her neck. She imagined the ring he'd gift her when she landed him gulping like a hooked trout. Not a silly emerald-cut, which didn't contain nearly enough facets to shine light off in all directions. How could she have thought her ring superior when the classic round solitaire best showed a diamond's brilliance?

"No matter," said she, "but my, what a shock, your appearance, though pleasant in the end." The perfect pause. "As I'm sure you can tell."

"Indeed," he said, and spied her erect nipples as proof. "It's too bad—"

"Yes?"

"Oh that, well—I suppose we'll need to discuss what you want from me." His pause rivaled hers for perfection. "During the wedding preparations, that is."

"Gracious, so many details to a wedding. We should confirm how you're to lay me down—rather, walk me down—the aisle."

They agreed on the hour for a *tête-a-tête* over tea. Eileen suggested old man Cashel's library on the other side of the manor, which, conveniently enough, contained a custom-made double-wide sofa and an inside lock.

IF YOU'RE picturing pretty Eileen a-straddle with her A-line skirt lifted, you'd be correct. Fast forward six hours into the evening with whiskey circulating and bawdy songs raised to the roof—the place was a proper drunken catastrophe by then—and you'd have witnessed that Eileen plying enough wares to make Gabriel's whore-moms proud.

Gabriel settled her on his lap snug enough, only too willing to grab his shag on the sly. However, was that a tinge of regret shadowing his eyes?

No, nothing but a wince as he adjusted his girth for an easier ride. He eyed the grandfather clock over Eileen's shoulder and grinned as she threw back her head with well-done groans of delight. She wasn't anywhere near a finale, and he for one didn't care because he had a timetable to keep. He hurried himself along until the world exploded and a satisfying limpness overtook him.

And just in time, Alan always adds when every bloke in The Deaf Justice sighs over the wondrous shudder that comes with the shag on the sly. Three, two, one, on the dot of 8:30 poor Evan burst into the room, Gabriel having previously unlocked the door while

Eileen peeled off her panty hose. "Thank Christ you had Shaunessy remind me to come along for a chat. I'm drunker than a—hmm—can't think of it now."

Any man with brains enough to fart would have sussed out the situation straight away. But not Evan, no. Not to ping too dearly on the wart, but how could he not interpret his Eileen's bare buttocks for anything but *coitus interruptus*?

"Huh?" he said. "What the—?"

To hasten Evan's brain cells along, Gabriel made haste to push Eileen off his lap. "Can't you leave a man alone?" he said with a perfect cry of remorse and regret. "Why, she's just using us, Brother!"

"Huh?" said she. "What the—?"

Fair Eileen, reduced to the stupidity of her fiancé. Her hanging jaw 'twas a sight to behold, that it was. Gabriel would have laughed if he weren't studying Evan's confusion, then denial, then hurt—then, thank Christ, outrage. After awhile even Evan couldn't mistake Eileen's sticky sprawl upon the oak floorboards.

YOU CAN imagine the rest: accusations, denials; insults, sweet nothings; rejection, tearful negotiations; and in the end, Gabriel and Evan, the closest of bachelor brothers to the end of their short-lived days. If Evan appeared sad at times, no one commented; if Gabriel, bitter, likewise. And if Evan never caught on that Gabriel played him for a dupe—he'd achieved *coitus completus*, after all—then no matter because he only meant to liberate his brother from that seductress Eileen.

Now it's three husbands later for Eileen, or so Alan claims, and she with a solitaire the size of a sheep's ball at that. It might be she's the one in the fox fur that visits the Rock now that the brothers have passed on—the one from syphilis caught during his gritty days, the other from blocked arteries. She of the fox fur, who's been heard to mutter, *Impossible, how did they both fit?* while pulling a tape measure out of her purse.

Down at The Deaf Justice, Alan still wonders aloud what might have become of the Cashel family had Evan landed himself a kind-hearted and homely lass, the type with modesty to bring home to ma and servility to bring home to da. Some argue that Gabriel would have tolerated such a piece of furniture, and Evan happily married might have swayed him toward ritualized monogamy himself.

And then who knows? To this day, you might be seeing family heirs around the village rather than two bachelor brothers laid out side by side up at the Rock of Cashel.

Lisa Alber the author of *Kilmoon*, an atmospheric mystery set in Ireland that has been described as "utterly poetic" and a "stirring debut." The novel was a Rosebud Award finalist for best debut novel. Lisa worked with *New York Times* bestselling author Elizabeth George in several workshops, which culminated in receiving an Elizabeth George Foundation writing grant. She is also a Walden Fellowship recipient and Pushcart Prize nominee. .The second novel in the series, *Whispers in the Mist* will be available August 2016 (Midnight Ink). She is currently at work on her third novel. She lives in the Pacific Northwest with a tiny dog and a chubby cat. You can find her online at www.lisaalber.com.

The Premature Wake of Michael Maloney

Alan M. Clark

Portland, Oregon 1882

LEANING OVER THE EDGE OF THE DECK, Police Officer Michael Maloney chuckled as he watched the dead man in the white suit bob up and down in the river current against the hull of the giant barge. The good humor came more from relief than anything else. He'd never thought he'd be able to shoot a man, and feared the day—this day—when he'd be faced with the decision to defend his life by taking another.

A little drink was all it took, Maloney thought. "And now you're in the drink," he whispered to the corpse. Laughing out loud, his left foot slipped out from under him and he nearly went into the water himself.

He sat to catch his breath and allowed his legs to dangle over the edge of the deck. The raid on the vessel was winding down. The other officers had corralled the prostitutes, the toughs, and their bosses. Time for another drink. Maloney was going for his flask when he heard rapid footsteps on the deck approaching and felt a hand reach for him.

Officer Douglas pulled Maloney upright on the deck and gave

him a look of outrage. "Why'd you shoot him?"

"You saw it," Maloney said, his words slurred. "He came for me with a knife. We've needed an excuse to be rid of Coorsey, and he gave it to me, the stupid lout!" He laughed again.

Officer Dunlevy was hanging over the side, using a boat hook to try and snag the corpse and turn it over.

"That's not Coorsey," Douglas said. "Whoever he is, you shot him in the back. Turns out, Coorsey wasn't here tonight."

Of course it's Coorsey, Maloney thought. No one else wore those precious white suits. The criminal boss had stepped out of a cabin suddenly and come for Maloney with a weapon. "The shot must've gone all the way through," he said.

He leaned over for another look just as Dunlevy got the body rolled over. Maloney saw no bullet hole in the chest or abdomen of the corpse. The face wasn't that of the criminal boss.

Maloney began to choke on his glee. He coughed and sputtered, reviewing his memories of just moments before, when the man swung out of the cabin door. Had he been holding something other than a knife? Was the man moving away instead of coming toward him? With the frequent nips of whiskey Maloney had had through-out the evening, he knew his perception was compromised and that his reaction time was off, but the mistake was beyond belief.

"You're drunk," Douglas said. "Put your pistol away."

Maloney still held the warm firearm. He holstered it. Of course he was drunk. He would never have been able to kill a man mechanically as some of the other officers did without a snootful. Maloney knew he wasn't well-suited for the work. He would never have got the job if not for his father, Robert Maloney, who had been a Sergeant in the Portland Oregon Police Department, until he was killed when his own horse kicked him in the head. Guys like Douglas had no compunction about dispatching criminals on the street when they feared the gears of justice would grind too slowly to do any good. They carried extra weapons with them to place with their victims to make the killings look like they were committed in self defense.

"Too many witnesses," Douglas said in answer to Maloney's un-asked question about the possibility of placing a knife on the man. "This guy's a nobody. He's soft, like he works in an office somewhere. He wouldn't have been foolish enough to attacked a policeman during a raid. Who would believe that?"

"I did," Maloney said pitifully.

"Yeah, well you're a fucking drunk, aren't you? Not fit for the police department." The disgust on Douglas's face was devastating. "Leave," he said. "Go home. I'll see what I can do about this, but I don't think I can fix it this time. The poor bastard is probably a family man out here for a romp with his whore, nothing more."

Maloney nodded his head. He had to get away from the scene. He had to get away from his response to seeing the man tumble overboard, his delight at the man's death. He fled his own drunken laughter, yet it pursued him along the deck.

Too many people, officers and those from the barge, stood in his way. He couldn't see himself sitting calmly in one of the dinghies with others as they were rowed slowly to shore. The nearest bank was only a hundred yards away. On impulse, he leapt overboard and began swimming.

He ignored the surprised responses of those behind him, and a couple of questions thrown his way. All he could think about was what his wife would think. Mary had seen him through so much lately, so many silly episodes with his drinking and some that were much worse than mere foolishness. Like running over the little negro girl with the police van. As she fell beneath hooves and wheels, her expression became frozen in his memory like a tintype, yet no photograph could capture an image so quickly nor represent it with such contrast and clarity. The bright rectangles of the girl's teeth in her screaming mouth, the white circles of her startled eyes against dark skin haunted him when he closed his eye.

"You didn't mean to harm the little girl," Mary had said. He winced. "She'll never walk again."

Mary caressed his troubled brow. "It was an accident."

He would never tell her how much he'd drunk while on duty that day, yet he was certain she knew he hadn't been sober.

"I must clean myself up and drink less," he said. "I must discipline myself before it's too late."

"You're not an angry or maudlin drunk," she said. "You're quite sweet when you've had a dram."

The fun was long gone from drinking, however. Maloney had been miserable with it for well over a year. He tried to lay off the sauce, and his desire seemed to stalk him and strike when he was weakest. Last month, he'd spent and entire week without a drink, experiencing the shakes and a bad gut through most of it. He'd tried several times before to quit and always failed. Though his shame was compounded each time he took it up again, he'd been grateful to have Mary stick by him.

But what would she say this time? He could only imagine her abhorrence, her rejection if she found out how he'd reacted to the man's death tonight; how he'd laughed. He couldn't face her. No, he couldn't go home.

When he pulled himself ashore, his laughter was not far behind him. As it chased him through the waterfront and into the streets between warehouses further from the river, he knew there was no escape without leaving his life behind.

Portland was known for its shanghai trade. Most of those who went missing weren't killed. Years later, some returned from the sea and told tales of how their lives were irrevocably altered. Although most were drunkards, ne'er-do-wells who were angry about what happened to them, Maloney had met a man named Ross who had been abducted and spent ten years away. He was a rather successful businessman with his own hardware store in the district where Maloney started as a beat cop seven years earlier.

"I'd been a drunkard when I was abducted," Ross had told him. "Even though I struggled to get back to my family and friends in Portland, the experience was the best thing that could've happened to me. It straightened me out. I got sober, and it helped me to value life as never before."

If Maloney were lucky enough to have such an experience he'd be fortunate, yet that wasn't perhaps what he deserved.

Let the city determine my fate, he decided, *since I don't have the guts or the willpower to change my life on my own. I've earned whatever might be dished up.*

Turning onto a busy street full of night life, Michael Maloney resolved to disappear into the dark heart of Portland and see where that took him.

Most of those who went missing didn't choose to disappear, but how hard could it be? A certain lack of awareness should help. Maloney had become good at that. He'd have to change out of his uniform and get rid of his pistol.

Brainard's Tavern was the first bar he came to. Maloney was acquainted with the owner of the establishment, Jack Brainard, a burley fellow with a streak of vanity. Entering the tavern, Maloney saw the man behind the bar, counting his receipts. Brainard had a head full of dark oily curls, perfectly combed, and a short black beard and mustache. His brown plaid ditto suit suggested that his vanity knew the limits of his budget. Although he wasn't rich, he was successful. He might purchase Maloney's revolver for cash and perhaps a change of clothes.

With a little money in his pocket, Maloney would head for an establishment where he was less known. He'd lose himself to alcohol and drugs and find a much craved state of forgetfulness. Sufficiently intoxicated, he wouldn't feel a thing when the cudgel descended upon his head or the trap door opened beneath him and he landed in the Shanghai tunnels beneath the city. When he woke up far out to sea, he'd miss Mary. She'd be better off without him, though. Regrets would follow, but the forced labor onboard the ship would give him little time for deep reflection. He could imagine that as he rounded the globe and disembarked somewhere in Asia, he'd become a new man, just as had happened for Mr. Ross. Maloney would leave his old life behind. He'd put away his shame and start anew without the sins of his past.

Brainard looked up as Maloney approached and said, "I'd like to sell my pistol."

The barkeep looked at him silently for a moment, then motioned for Maloney to join him in a storeroom down a short hall from the bar.

Having sold the pistol and donned the mildewed clothes Brainard gave him, Maloney headed west toward Chinatown and entered another bar, one he'd never visited before. After consuming ten shots of whiskey, he began a prolonged blackout and was unaware of his own activities for the next few days.

THREE DAYS after his attempted disappearance, Mary and her four brothers located Maloney in an opium den in Chinatown. They hauled him unconscious back home.

When he awoke, night had descended outside his bedroom window. Mary sat by the bedside reading a book by lamplight. She saw him stir and called to her brothers. All four crowded into the small room, each wearing the same warm Cleary smile.

The five clustered about Maloney were his family. He had no other.

Conall, the oldest, set a bottle of whiskey on the dresser. "I expect you'll be needing a little of this if you want to avoid the shakes," he said.

Maloney nodded sadly.

"You have a fool's luck," Brian said, and the other Cleary men nodded.

Maloney shook his head. "I'll lose my job."

"'Tis lost already," Sean said, shrugging wistfully.

Mary reached for Maloney's hand and gave it a warm squeeze. "Officer Douglas came by and told me to tell you not to come in," she said.

"How is that luck, then?" he asked.

"The luck is that we found you before it was too late," Brian said, "before you were shipped out to sea."

"Word is," Conall said, "the man who died in the raid on the whiskey barge was the philandering husband of a socialite who doesn't want the case dragged through the courts and her name in the newspapers. They're saying he fell in the river and drowned."

"Still, it's bad luck for Mary," Maloney said. "I do her little good, and now, without work, I'm good for nothing."

Conall placed a hand on Maloney's shoulder. "We'll help you get by until you find work."

Whereas most in-laws might have felt differently, the Cleary brothers were all hard-drinking men like Maloney. He had been their drinking pal since before he took an interest in their sister.

"If it weren't for Mary, we might not have found you," Patrick said. "The four of us, blundering around town looking for you, stirred up a lot of trouble. She insisted on going with us to Chinatown. The Chinamen have ways of keeping their clients safely hidden. Some of their toughs came after us, but Mary got between us and them. She shamed them into letting us pass."

"What did you say?" Maloney asked.

Mary lowered her gaze as if ashamed. "It's not important."

"She said," Conall answered, "I won't leave until I've searched for my husband. If you must stop me, will you then boast that you beat a woman?"

Mary shook her head. "They *would* have beat me," she said, "I'm certain of that."

"We hadn't thought to tell them you were a policeman because by then you'd been sacked," Conall said.

"I figured they wouldn't know," Mary said. "I told them you were a police officer and they let us be."

Maloney looked at his wife with tenderness and a tear came to his eye. While contemplating the scenario of his own shanghaiing, he'd known that once he was gone she was all he'd regret.

"Let's leave the lovebirds alone," Patrick said, tugging on Conall's sleeve and heading for the door.

"Thanks for looking out for me," Maloney said.

"Not at all," Conall said. The brothers nodded, smiled, and filed out.

Mary looked at Maloney with concern, and poured him a drink. "sip it slowly," she said.

Maloney wiped his brimming tears and lifted the glass of whiskey to his lips.

DESPITE THE love of a good woman—and in large part because of it—Maloney's drinking worsened. He had no regular employment after losing his position with the Portland Police department. What work he found, he could not keep because of his habit. If not for Mary's four brothers, they would have been destitute.

"A good thing we had no luck bringing children into the world," Maloney told Conall.

"You shouldn't talk like that," Conall said. "You'll get your bearings. Then, you'll see, everything will work out with you and Mary."

What does he know? Maloney thought. What did any of the Cleary brothers know? A bunch of drunks was what they were, although they all seemed capable of handling their alcohol while keeping their jobs. Still, not a one of them knew anything about married life. None of them had ever had a steady girl. When a Cleary needed a woman, he looked for a whore.

IN THE following two years of Maloney's unemployment, he and Mary accepted financial assistance from her brothers. Being dock-side workers, the Cleary Brothers were not rich. Although Michael didn't feel good about taking their money, yet did so for Mary's sake. Since he was in charge of the funds that came to them, he used some of it to buy alcohol. As time passed, the amount of the funds he used for drink increased until it was the lion's share, and there was little left for food. The thinner Mary became, the worse he felt about himself. Finally, Maloney could not live with the situation any longer. He waited until a Saturday when the brothers were visiting and announced that he was leaving Mary.

"You can't abandon her" Conall said. "That would be most cruel."

No," Maloney said, "the real cruelty to her is what I have made of her loving husband. If I can't control my drinking—and clearly I cannot—then I shouldn't benefit from your generosity and pity, nor hers" he told the brothers. "Mary deserves your assistance. I surely do not. I know that you will look out for her."

They protested and Mary tearfully begged him to stay, but Maloney was adamant.

"No," Mary sobbed, "you'll get better. I love you, Michael."

Fearing that if he responded his resolve would crumble, Maloney did not trust himself to say another word. He had packed a few articles of clothing into a carpet bag. He took the bag from where he'd hidden it in a wardrobe, and headed out the door, Mary clutching at him and wailing, her brothers trying to pull her away. Michael knew the Cleary brothers understood.

Until he found work, Maloney stayed in a shelter provided for the unemployed homeless by the Methodist Church. He took what odd jobs he could find, running errands or hauling goods for businesses downtown. Much of the work occurred underground, through secret tunnels that ran under the streets, connecting the basements of buildings, connecting many establishments to loading areas at the waterfront.

Maloney lived in a flophouse when he could afford it. In warm weather, he slept outdoors or in various unfinished tunnels and niches within the underground that were considered a cave-in risk and therefore rarely visited by others.

On and off, he wished to be shanghaied, if for no other reason than to shake up his world, to force him into some sort of change, hopefully like what had happened for Mr. Ross. But it didn't happen, despite the fact that no one would mistake him for a police officer any longer. One day, looking at himself in a mirror, he realized that in his condition, no one who engaged in the shanghai trade would consider him a commodity worth selling. Thin and raggedy as he was, life had given him all that he deserved.

"What do you think is the most painless way to end life?" he'd asked the Cleary brothers one evening while they sat drinking.

"We won't be entertaining that subject," Conall said with a huff. His three brother shook their heads slowly.

"Would be a sin," Sean said with a sigh.

Maloney wasn't certain he had the guts to go through with it anyway.

THREE YEARS after the whiskey barge raid, Maloney worked for Brainard much of the time. He'd had two bouts with DTs on occasions when he didn't earn enough to maintain his habit. Both times he'd spent a week in Morningside Hospital recovering, then returned immediately to drinking when he got out.

In September, 1885, on an occasion when the barkeep was away for the night, Maloney slept off a binge in a dark corner of the tavern storeroom. He awoke hung over. The cup of broth that he was eating prior to falling insensible, horse stock he'd stolen from the kitchen, was upset on the upturned barrel he'd used as a table.

Next to the cup was a bottle of whiskey. Without thinking about how it got there, he reached for it to help quiet the throb in his head and the sickening turn of his gut. As his hands were about to close around it, he saw that Brian Cleary was holding the bottle in place and hadn't removed his hand from its neck yet. Although Maloney could think of little but the hair-of-the-dog remedy, he lowered his hands as respect demanded that he wait until his buddy offered him a drink. Noting that all four of the Cleary lads were assembled in the storeroom with eager expressions, he knew such an invitation would be forthcoming.

"We've got a plan that'll help Mary," Conall said, and all three of his brothers nodded, their eyes wide with approval.

That got Maloney's attention.

"We know you don't like Mr. Brainard," Sean said. "Though it's his plan, hear us out because it might be the answer to our prayers."

"I'm all ears," Maloney said. Still, he was instantly suspicious of any scheme concocted by Brainard. The barkeep pushed him around unnecessarily and seemed to enjoy it. Maloney had discovered the man's shanghai trap while mucking out one of the tavern's privies. A catch prevented the seat and interior side walls of the stall from tipping backwards. Maloney had accidentally triggered it while cleaning. As the seat and walls tipped back suddenly, a gap over a ten foot drop was revealed. Not being seated on the contraption, Maloney's weight was squarely on his legs and feet against the floor, and he avoided falling in. He righted the apparatus, secured it with the catch and said nothing about it.

Maloney had known that Brainard was a bad man. Even so, he would listen to the Cleary brothers since they would not agree to anything that might harm him or their beloved sister.

"We take out a life insurance policy on you," Patrick said. "We all"—he indicated himself and his three brothers—"chip in half on the monthly premium and Brainard the other half. He opens the tap for you—as much as you can drink for as long as it takes to…well, you know. Then, when you've…uh, passed on, he gets half, and we give our half to Mary. Whatever happens, it must look natural. The insurance company will not pay for a suicide. Meanwhile, you don't have to do any work around the tavern, and you can sleep in the storeroom."

Although Maloney had difficulty thinking past the part about the open tap at first, he sat in silence for a time, considering the motivations of those who would be involved in the plot.

The Cleary brothers had listened to him talk about taking his own life for some time. Maloney had made the mistake of allowing Brainard to overhear him talk about suicide, and his concern for Mary's financial state on one occasion. At first, his pals had tried to dissuade Maloney from even thinking about taking his own life. Slowly, though, their dismissive expressions had turned to those of sympathy. Maloney believed they'd come to recognize the suffering in his eyes. They all knew that Mary suffered for knowing what had become of the husband she still loved.

Concerning Brainard's part in the scheme—well, he was a greedy man, but as long as there was a profit to be had, he'd keep his side of an agreement.

A smile grew on Maloney's face, despite the pain in his noggin. "Yes, I'll go along with the plan."

Conall had been right when he'd said Maloney had a fool's luck. For all the perils of his chronic drinking, he'd found love with Mary, and still had the respect of her family. That had made the misery of life worthwhile until the present. Now, unable to escape the clutches of strong drink, he would find it to be his salvation. He imagined that with an open tap at Brainard's Tavern he might drink himself to death quickly and with little or no pain.

AT LEAST one of the Cleary brothers came to Brainard's Tavern each night that the tap was open to Maloney. Many nights they were all there. Maloney tried not to ask after Mary, yet could not help himself on a few occasions.

"We don't tell her anything about our time with you," Brian said. "If she asks if we've seen you, we lie."

"That is right and proper," Michael said.

* * *

AT FIRST the drinking Maloney and the Cleary Brothers did at Brainard's Tavern had a celebratory aspect to it.

"A toast to our good friend and brother, Michael Maloney," Conall said. "He was a fine man, and a good friend with a big heart. He made our sister happy and brought good cheer into our lives." Conall was drunk, yet seemed to realize he'd spoken of Maloney in the past tense. He smiled sheepishly at his friend.

"Not to worry," Maloney said. "This *is* my wake. I am already a dead man, and better off for it." He laughed and quaffed a mug of beer.

"We intend to see you off and on to the next world in style," Brian said. His brothers cheered and drank.

Conall's toast was only the first of many the brothers would give Maloney.

Brainard had given them a table in a back corner, but soon saw that his other patrons had a positive reaction to the pals' drunken frolics, and moved their table closer to the front of the tavern.

"You boys keep it up," Brainard told them. "Your gaiety is driving the ghosts from the place." Then he turned to Maloney, "You tell anyone who asks that you won the open tap for saving the life of my sister in Tahiti, and if anyone should wish to buy you a drink, it'll be on the house."

That brought a riotous cheer from those at the table. Word spread quickly over the next week, and patrons vied to see just what and just how much they could get Maloney to drink each night. He downed many different vile concoctions, smiling as he did so for an audience that grew nightly. No matter what he drank, the effect seemed to be the same. The Cleary brothers cheered him on. He took brief breaks to be ill. He pissed himself and soiled his pants as he sat with his pals. The brothers didn't care. They would celebrate his life until they couldn't any longer. If he was unavailable or unconscious for a time, the party seemed to go on without him until he could catch up again.

Generally, he was unaware of the end of each evening; how he got back to the storeroom to sleep it off. He arose mid-afternoon of the each day, stumble to the kitchen, and fetched himself broth from a pot that always stood steaming on the stove.

On rare occasion, with inevitable denial, he wondered how he'd gotten into such a sad state. He had fallen so far in such a short time! Upon little reflection, though, he saw the path clearly.

As the drunken revels escalated over the weeks, Brainard stood apart from it smiling. Maloney thought he did so rather smugly. Liking the fellow had never been important, and soon he would not have to look at the man's ugly face any longer.

Maloney figured that any night the poison he poured into himself would become too much and his body would fail. He hoped that when that occurred, he'd be asleep in the storeroom, that his passing would be painless, and his friends wouldn't have to witness it. As the weeks passed into months, he ceased to worry about it. He was having a good time with his friends.

Brainard's smug expression changed as he watched the activities at Maloney's table over time. The novelty of the Maloney table had run its course for the clientele of the tavern. The celebratory aspect had also wound down slowly, the Cleary brothers inventing fewer toasts to fill the atmosphere with glee. Brainard ceased to smile. His features took on a peevish look that spoke of patience worn threadbare, and eventually settled into an expression of hateful intolerance. One might have thought the barkeep was looking at a pile of excrement that offended his patrons but which could not be cleaned up.

One morning, three months into the open tap bargain, Maloney awoke and went to the kitchen for his broth and found Brainard waiting for him. When Maloney reached for the ladle to pour a cup, the barkeep blocked him.

"You're taking too long," he said. "You're costing us all a lot of money. I can't keep paying the premiums forever."

"I'm trying my best," Maloney said. "Have you ever seen a man drink like I have done?"

"Regardless," Brainard said, "you'll have to start compensating me by doing work around the place."

Maloney, hung over as usual, was in no condition for labor. "There's isn't much I can do," he said weakly.

"You'll have no broth unless you muck out the privies each day."

Maloney did as he was told. Over the next few weeks, Brainard demanded that Maloney take on numerous new daily chores.

A MONTH later, in the middle of December, Brainard dragged the unconscious Maloney from the storeroom at about three o'clock in the morning and told him he could no longer sleep in his establishment. "Perhaps if you stay out in the cold, you'll freeze to death," the barkeep said. He shoved Maloney out the door of the tavern, giving him a swift kick in the ass. Maloney tumbled into the street. The temperature was well below freezing. Hoof prints in the mud were rimmed with dirty ice. Maloney sat up and looked back. "What about the open tap?"

"That's only good when the Tavern is open. Come back with your pals later. At least you bring me their business."

At the late hour, the businesses that Maloney had served when he'd run errands through the underground were all closed, so he lacked access to the tunnels through all but one entry; a bent metal gate that covered the entrance to a partially caved-in passage at the waterfront. Poorly dressed for the weather as he was, he hurried for the shelter, hoping he was still thin enough to pass between the bars.

He was surprised to find that he was thinner than ever. The temperature inside the tunnel wasn't much warmer than outside. He made his way deeper, feeling his way along the wall for the little alcove he used to hole up in during warm weather. His hands found an opening in the wall and he reached inside and felt around. Feeling something furry, he drew back, startled and fearing an angry animal attack. When nothing came after him, he reached in again. The fur belonged to a large dog, its body stiffened in rigor mortis. No strong odor came from the dead animal. No doubt it had crawled off there to die within the last couple of days and the cold weather had slowed its decomposition. Maloney decided that the fur would help protect him from the cold. He crawled into the alcove and drew the dead beast into a warming embrace.

BRAINARD WAS true to his word. He allowed Maloney back into the tavern at noon when the establishment reopened.

"You tell your pals about my change in our agreement and I'll back out of the whole thing," The barkeep said. "Where will your sweet Mary be then?"

Maloney feared the look of resolve in the man's eyes. He nodded his head.

"THERE'S ALREADY seven inches of snow on the ground," Conall said as they sat with their drinks that evening. He was the only Cleary brother to join Maloney that night. He lived the closest to the tavern. "It's well below freezing already and the temperature will drop more."

Maloney wanted to ask Conall if he could stay the night with him, but he remembered the look in Brainard's eyes.

Sailors say that dying in the cold is rather peaceful, he reminded himself. *Could be worse.* He kept his mouth shut when he wasn't laughing with his pal and downing his drinks.

MALONEY CAME awake briefly late at night, just long enough to realized that Brainard had chucked him out the back door of the tavern into a snow drift in the alley.

This is it, he told himself. *I'm done for, and it's about time.* He rolled over and closed his eyes.

* * *

WHEN MALONEY walked in the tavern at noon the next day, the look of astonishment on Brainard's face expressed just what Maloney felt about his own continued existence.

"That's it," the barkeep shouted. "I must talk to the Cleary boys about drastic measures."

He stomped off and Maloney began work on his chores as the pins and needles of returning circulation within his tissues drove him crazy.

A MONTH later, the Cleary brothers were all gathered to see him off. Brainard had persuaded them to serve Maloney a poisonous concoction. They had prepared a boilermaker with two heaping helpings of rat poison.

"Just drink it fast," Patrick said.

As Maloney raised the drink to his lips, the brothers all cringed. He almost set the glass down to save their feelings, but knew they'd just have to try again. They were all invested in the outcome, with their sister, Maloney's loving wife, the beneficiary.

He quickly quaffed the terrible brew.

AGAIN, HE awoke in the alley. He was covered in kitchen refuse. Brainard had tossed him out with the trash, no doubt confident that this time, Maloney would not rise again. He had a stomach ache and terrific hangover. His mouth was dry and gummy, and he was seeing cross-eyed. He rose and stumbled around to the front of the building, having to feel his way because of his confusing vision. The tavern was closed. He sat on the covered wooden footway that wrapped around the front of the building, leaned against a support post and waited.

He awoke with a start and a severe pain in his thigh. Brainard had arrived and given him another swift kick.

"YOU CAN'T just have him thrown in the river," Conall said

to Brainard.

"Then we shove him into the street under one of the big team-ster's rigs," the Barkeep shouted.

Brainard's office was too small for such loud voices. Maloney covered his ears with his hands to shut out the painful sounds. His eyesight had recovered and he watched the altercation feeling rather detached, as if they couldn't possibly be talking about how to kill him. After all, four of the five men involved were his best friends.

"I know something that's supposed to be deadly indeed," Sean said. "Raw oysters soaked in wood alcohol. We can get the ingredients and in a few days make another go of it."

Some effort was required to get Brainard calmed down enough to agree. When the matter was finally settled, Sean said he knew where he could get oysters and left. Brainard said he had wood alcohol.

He probably serves it to customer he doesn't like, Maloney decided. Then he laughed out loud at the thought. *Like me!*

He could see that the laughter had set Brainard's blood to boiling again. Patrick and Brian quickly ushered Maloney out of the office.

THE BROTHERS gave encouragement as Maloney downed one oyster after another, yet their expressions belied their positive words. With each foul-tasting gray lump he swallowed, they cringed. Sean turned away to gag twice. "They're like the fishy snot balls of a whale," Maloney said, laughing and trying to get his pals to smile. He couldn't pull it off. The pain in their eyes was plain to see. They truly loved him, but seeing that he was indeed lost, they had embarked with him on the dark journey to his death to help their poor sister.

Yes, the pain in their eyes was clear as day. Maloney was certain the same was true of Mary. His death must come soon for the sake of those he loved.

Perhaps tonight, in my sleep. He downed another oyster.

* * *

MALONEY DID not die that night. When Brainard saw him alive the next day, he lifted Maloney by the shoulders. "I am the only one with a signature on the insurance documents," the barkeep said, smashing Michael against the wall of the storeroom. His words, short and sharp, crackled with frustration and barely contained rage. "You will help your friends find a way to end this right away, or I'll have you killed and keep all the proceeds."

"No," Maloney said, "you have a bargain with the Cleary boys. My wife—"

Brainard had walked out, slamming the storeroom door behind him. He wasn't just a bad man. He was evil. Maloney should have understood that when he'd found the man's shanghai trap. Although clearly the barkeep made his threat because he was reaching for leverage, Maloney was now certain the man had intended to keep all of the insurance payout from the start, whatever happened. He had duped the Cleary brothers and Maloney. Mary would never benefit from the insurance policy.

Michael remembered comparing himself to officer Douglas and his like, men who could mechanically dispatch justice on the street with a pistol. "You have to do it without feeling," Douglas had told him once. "You must do it mechanically." Maloney hadn't been able to kill without alcohol to dampen his conscience. He wanted to believe that if he were still a policeman, had the chance to dispatch Brainard, and cover it up with a dropped weapon, he'd do it without a second thought. He knew that wasn't true, though. More than ever, the thought of killing a man troubled him.

He might not be able to kill Brainard, but Maloney sure could foil the barkeep's plot with an apparent suicide. Whatever happened, he was confident that the Cleary brothers would take care of Mary.

Michael stepped out of the storeroom. The Tavern hadn't opened. Brainard was nowhere in sight. The barkeep kept the pistol Maloney had sold him three years earlier in a drawer behind the bar.

Michael would have it back briefly.

He retrieved the pistol, walked out the front door of Brainard's Tavern and stood with the warm midday sun on his face for a moment as he watched the traffic along the busy street. Then, he raised the pistol to his head, waited until pedestrians had become curious enough to watch him, and pulled the trigger.

MALONEY SLOWLY became aware that he was alive.

His head hurt, particularly on the right side.

He drifted in and out of consciousness.

THE PAIN in his head increased. He thought to try to sooth it with a caress of his hand and found he couldn't move.

His vision was distorted and unfocused, yet seemed to be improving.

He drifted off again, and when later he awoke, he felt a weak connection to his body. As that slowly became stronger, he discovered nothing but pain. His gut cramped in withdrawal spasms, his flesh was fevered, seething with heat and chills that crept across his skin and through his muscle tissues. His viscera began to revolt, the organs seeming to writhe painfully within his chest and abdomen. His heart beat against his chest so fast and hard he expected it might break out. As his body quaked, he could feel it straining against the straps that bound him to the surface upon which he lay. He became aware that he had soiled himself and was sopping wet with sweat and perhaps urine.

His vision cleared enough that he could see he was in a small, green room. In the dark corners near the ceiling, small black insects bred at a furious pace among the cracked plaster.

Maloney understood that he was suffering delirium tremens. With his earlier experiences with DTs, he recognized the hallucinations. He also recognized the room as one belonging to Morningside Hospital. Perhaps it was one he'd occupied during an earlier episode.

The offspring of the insects became larger and larger, the bigger eating the smaller. Some escaped being eaten as they became interested in Maloney and explored every inch of him. One settled on his forehead and right temple and became still.

In some way he could not identify, the previous experience had been much more difficult. Although he could not control his heart, his spasmodic motions, and the flashes of fever through his system, he knew somehow that with time, the excruciating pain and other symptoms would pass. And so they did over the course of what must have been several days, during which the insect on Maloney's head remained where it was, undisturbed.

A man in white came in to clean Maloney up three times during that period. On his fourth visit, he was accompanied by a physician. The doctor made a quick examination of Maloney. He asked the man in white to tighten one of the straps. Then he leaned over and concentrated on Maloney's head. He gingerly plucked at the insect draped across Maloney's forehead and temple, then carefully lifted it. The insect, as seen in Maloney's peripheral vision, appeared to have turned red and white. Once the insect was removed, the doctor probed the surface of Maloney's forehead and temple.

"You're a lucky man," he said. "The bullet went all the way through."

The physician wound a bandage onto Maloney's head, then left. The bandage felt much the same as the insect had.

Time passed in what seemed several more days.

"I UNDERSTAND you are a married man, Mr. Maloney," The doctor said on his second visit.

Maloney was sitting up in his bed. The straps had been removed. "Yes," he said, and it was the first word he'd spoken since the injury. Although his thought processes were a bit slow, his memories were returning. His understanding seemed different, but he couldn't say how.

"She has tried to see you, and expects you to come home today. You are indeed a lucky man."

The physician had removed the bandage from Maloney's head. He held up a mirror. Maloney hardly recognized his thin and pale face. Two large scabs stood out on his head, one at his right temple and another one, seeping a small amount of pink fluid, on the left side of his forehead.

"I was a field surgeon during the War Between the States," the doctor said. "I saw soldiers who suffered similar wounds. They were men I had known before and after their injuries. Some I kept in touch with to see how they progressed." He set down the mirror and looked Maloney in the eye. "If you are like those men, your life will be very different from what it was before your injury. You will be able to work, and, God willing, your wife will help keep you. You may find that you lack motivation because you are emotionally detached. I understand that you had a severe drinking habit before. You may now lack all desire for it. The feelings that accompany our likes and dislikes propel us to most of our decision-making. You may find that your wife or whoever might employ you will be required to make decisions for you. You should have no difficulty with this. Your life will go on and you should live out your days as healthy and physically able as any other man."

The doctor might as well have been talking to someone else for all the pertinence his words had for Maloney, but perhaps that was because Michael was distracted by a thought, one that he voiced. "Without drink, I can be a police officer," Maloney said. "I must provide for my wife."

The doctor looked at him with surprise. "That's very good," he said, "extraordinary, in fact. Perhaps you have retained some ability to motivate yourself. It is a good sign that you may have a fuller recovery than the men I've known in the past. But perhaps you should set your sights a bit lower until you've got your footing."

The doctor paused for a moment, then said, "Your former employer, Mr. Brainard, has contacted us and offered to deliver you to your wife. He will pick you up at the entrance to the hospital in fifteen minutes."

Brainard wants me dead, Maloney thought.

"An orderly will escort you down stairs in a moment." The doctor got to his feet. "Please stand."

Maloney stood. The doctor bent and picked something up that had been resting beside his chair. "Here are the possession that accompanied you to Morningside. I wish you a good life, Mr. Maloney."

He shook Michael's hand, turned and walked out of the room as a man, dressed in white, entered.

The cloth sack the doctor had handed Maloney held threadbare, stained clothing, and his police revolver.

He knew what the weapon was for. He knew how the thing worked and that it was a tool policemen used.

Douglas and other officers used pistols to kill criminals.

Brainard was a criminal.

Maloney looked at the tips of the bullets remaining in the chambers of the pistol's cylinder and thought about seeing Brainard out front of the hospital.

Michael remembered not wanting to shoot criminals, even though it came with the job of policeman.

He remembered thinking about shooting the barkeep once before.

Something had stopped him at the time.

He lifted his right hand to probe the wound at his temple with a finger, searching for something.

The man dressed in white gently pulled Maloney's hand away from the wound. Holding him by the arm, the man led him out of the room and down several halls and a stairway to the entrance of the building. All the while, Michael examined his mind to identify what had stood in the way of his using the tool with the bullets in it, but he still couldn't put his finger on it.

Seeing Brainard waving to him from his carriage in the drive and thinking about shooting him, Michael knew that whatever had stood in the way was gone.

The man in white released him, and Michael continued toward the carriage. When he was close enough, he stopped, pulled the pistol from the sack, and aimed it at Brainard's head.

The barkeep's eyes and mouth grew large. He was trying to say something with his expression, but Michael could not understand what was being communicated, and there was little time to consider it before his finger squeezed the trigger.

Perhaps the lack of understanding is part of what the doctor was talking about, Maloney thought as a third eye opened in Brainard's face and the sound of the pistol going off echoed among the buildings of the hospital grounds.

The barkeep's face retreated as his body slumping backwards in the carriage seat.

The tiny kernel of Maloney's curiosity was short-lived. He and the pistol had both functioned properly—that was all the mattered.

Michael knew he was fit for the police department. He'd get his job back and provide for Mary. Life would go on, just as the doctor had said.

Alan M. Clark grew up in Tennessee in a house full of bones and old medical books. He has created illustrations for hundreds of books, including works of fiction of various genres, nonfiction, textbooks, young adult fiction, and children's books. Awards for his illustration work include the World Fantasy Award and four Chesley Awards. He is the author of 15 books, including eight novels, a lavishly illustrated novella, four collections of fiction, and a nonfiction full-color book of his artwork. His latest novel, *Say Anything But Your Prayers*, was released by Lazy Fascist Press in August 2014. He is an Associate Editor for Broken River Books, a Portland, Oregon publisher of crime fiction. Mr. Clark's company, IFD Publishing, has released 6 traditional books and 25 ebooks by such authors as F. Paul Wilson, Elizabeth Engstrom, and Jeremy Robert Johnson. Alan M. Clark and his wife, Melody, live in Oregon. www.alanmclark.com

A Darkquick Sky

Matthew Lowes

MAHENDRA SINGH STILL FELT the lingering after effects of transit cryosleep. At forty-eight, space travel had taken a toll on his aging body. His head ached and his joints were stiff, but his heart felt light as dawn broke over the edge of a new world. On *Magellan*'s exterior monitors, he watched as their low orbit brought them around the dark side of a moonless planet, and a red dwarf star rose above the horizon.

The faded picture of his wife and daughter, taped to the plastic of his control room console, seemed like an abstraction next the images of the new planet. No matter how many worlds he saw, Mahendra always succumbed to the romance of discovery. He became an explorer to satisfy an obsession that had haunted him since youth. He was always searching for new wonders, the secrets of the cosmos just beyond his grasp.

At times like this, he always wished these Space Authority starships had windows. The sunrise was spectacular, but there was no true dawn on the surface below. The planet SL283a was tidally locked to its parent star, one side in perpetual light, and the other fixed in a never-ending night.

Jessica Lee, the expedition's executive officer, came up behind him and leaned over his shoulder for a long kiss. Her skin smelled of marena-scented soap, a flower harvested at the colony on Naisa. The scent lingered in the air as she slid into the chair beside him and studied an image on one of the monitors. "What do you think that is?" she said, pointing at a swirling black mass visible at the edge of the planet's dark side.

"I don't know," Mahendra said. "Cloud formations perhaps."

"I've never seen anything like it." Jessica magnified the image. She traced a finger along a writhing tendril of black clouds that snaked out of the night. "It looks wrong somehow," she said, and her face contracted into an expression of disgust.

Mahendra turned his attention to the stream of data the ship's sensor arrays were churning out on the planet. Endless numbers scrolled down one screen, high definition images across another. He touched an image and expanded it, examining a swath of the terminus, the narrow zone between the light and dark sides of the planet. The light and dark sides were likely uninhabitable, due to extreme heat and cold. However, a thin band within the terminus could sustain habitable conditions.

Mahendra enlarged another image on the screen. Great patches of dark grey covered the twilight landscape of the terminus. "That's got to be some kind of vegetation down there. Science team will want to have a look at this."

Magellan carried a crew of six, including Captain Singh, which didn't seem like many considering the size of the ship and the extended duration of their expedition. But it was enough. The systems were automated, and the computer essentially flew the ship, making all the calculations for propulsion and hyperspace transfers.

They were two years out. It had taken them a full year in hyperspace, a year in cryosleep, just to reach this region. Then they had begun their explorations, traveling from one promising star system to another, searching for needles in the haystack of the galaxy, habitable worlds, valuable resources, and intelligent alien life. They collected data, named planets, and mostly moved on. If they found a planet worth further investigation, they could land in the dropship to make a thorough survey. On their last stop, they barely slowed down to make a few observations of three gas giants and the barren, icy moons orbiting them. Mahendra and Jessica didn't even wake the rest of the crew.

"The atmosphere is stable," Jessica said "just dense enough to move some heat around and keep the atmosphere from freezing up on the night side."

Mahendra watched her as she studied the data on her screen. The light from the monitor illuminating the features of her face. "Breathable?"

Jessica touched her screen, bringing up additional data. She raised her eyebrows and nodded. "A bit thin on oxygen, but it's within limits. And the terminus is quite temperate."

Mahendra hoped they could put off waking the others for a few days. He wanted to enjoy some more time alone with Jessica.

A flashing light on the console caught Jessica's attention. She tapped the screen with a finger. "Computer's picked up a signal."

"From where?"

Jessica's hands danced across the screen. "From the surface." She shrugged, as if she knew that couldn't be right. "I'm putting it on audio."

A series of tones crackled out of the speaker.

Mahendra's eyes narrowed as he listened to the sound. It repeated every few seconds. "Sounds like an old transponder beacon."

"But nobody else has been out this far."

They were passing across the terminus now, from night into day. The grey landscape that lay between was directly below them.

"Someone has." Mahendra pulled up the outdated transponder codes. "We used these on some of the mining freighters. It's an emergency signal, an old one." Mahendra shook his head. "That's why the computer didn't decode it."

"But—"

"Just a minute, I'm trying to locate the source…there."

A computer enhanced image revealed the fuzzy but undeniable outline of a old model VTOL dropship. It was difficult to tell what kind of condition it was in. They both stared at the screen in utter amazement.

"Do you realize what the odds are?" Jessica said.

"Get on the radio," Mahendra said. "See if you can contact anyone down there."

Jessica put on a headset and adjusted the radio transceiver. "This is Planetary Explorer Ship *Magellan*. Come in. Over."

Silence.

"This is Planetary Explorer Ship *Magellan*. Is there anybody there? Over."

More silence. Faint static.

Mahendra got up out of his seat. Jessica put a hand on his forearm. "Where are you going?"

"To wake the others."

THE BEIGE walls of the common room curved around the gathered crew. Still groggy-eyed from cryosleep, they listened to Mahendra's briefing with growing interest. The smell of strong coffee lent to a sense of morning, despite the ship's clock reading three in the afternoon.

Eckardt Blair, biologist and doctor, ran a hand through his thinning white hair. His pudgy lips curled in thought. "What ship could have even made it out here?"

"I looked into that," Jessica said. "There are three missing Planetary Explorer expeditions."

Chelsea Fleet, a young planetary scientist on her first expedition, gulped down the last of her coffee. "What about the system we bounced? You should have woken us. Even uninhabitable planets are of scientific interest."

Their dropship pilot, Fred "Mac" MacArdel, shook his head. "What's the point? So you can look at some screens? All the data is on file. Look, if we're not landing, don't wake us. I need my beauty sleep."

Jessica continued. "The Langston Expedition set out on a course in this direction. It's possible they could have made it this far, and if something went wrong, survived on the planet below."

"The Langston Expedition was over fifty years ago," Blair said. "Without extended cryosleep they would all be dead."

David Evans yawned. The engineer hadn't said a word until now. "That's not necessarily true. The old hyperspace navigation systems weren't nearly as accurate as the ones we have now. If something went wrong, the Langston Expedition could have spent significant time at relativistic speeds."

"Hmm," Blair said, scratching a three day beard that had actually been there for two months. "I suppose they could have had children as well. Relationships do happen."

Mahendra wondered if Blair knew about him and Jessica, and just as quickly decided he didn't care. "Either way, we need to prep the dropship for an immediate landing."

"Wait a minute," Chelsea said. "You want to land immediately? We barely know anything about this planet. Look, I'm not saying we don't go down there, but whatever happened to them could happen to us. Isn't it better to wait until we know more?"

"That ship didn't crash," Mahendra said. "It landed there, and there could be survivors. I worked on mining freighters for years before joining the Planetary Explorers, and I've been around some accidents. Every second counts when you're stranded on an alien world. Until we know more, this is a rescue mission."

"I'm concerned about those dark cloud formations on the night side," Jessica said. "some of them extend out toward the landing area. I've never seen clouds quite like that."

"Clouds aren't a problem," Mac said. "It's wind that's a bitch."

MAHENDRA SEALED his adaptive environmental suit and climbed

one of the ladders that led up to the hub. A central shaft ran the length of *Magellan*, from the primary engines at one end to the hyperspace transfer casing at the other. The rest of the crew was already onboard and prepping the dropship.

As he climbed, the modicum of pseudo-gravity they enjoyed in the rotating habitat lessened, and he became increasingly weightless. Climbing turned to graceful bounds, and bounding turned to floating upward with the slightest pull of his hand. When he reached the middle of the ship he pulled himself into the central shaft.

Beyond the confines of the habitat, the industrial nature of these Space Authority ships became apparent. The lighting was minimal, the air stale and cold, and the shaft itself was as much a central nervous system for the ship as it was a passageway for the crew. Masses of pipes and conduits ran the length of the dimly lit shaft. The tunnel was dizzyingly long.

Mahendra floated toward the front of *Magellan* along a line of metal handholds. Several tunnels radiated off the central core, providing access to the cargo holds and the dropship hangar. He pirouetted, upended himself, and dove down the nearest tunnel. Descending effortlessly into the dropship ready room, he executed a midair 180 degree turn and touched down lightly on the floor.

Old style pressure suits, helmets, and equipment lined the walls. A sealed airlock on one wall led out to the hanger, while the open airlock on the floor was mated to the top hatch of the dropship. Mahendra looked around briefly, then floated down through the hatch and sealed everything behind him.

The crew could live and work in the dropship for extended periods. The ship had its own common room, a science lab, crew quarters, and a ready room at the lower airlock. But everything was tiny, cramped, and stripped down to the bare essentials.

In the cockpit, the crew were already strapped into their seats and busy running over last minute preparations. Mahendra caught a glance of Chelsea's face through her visor as he passed. She was sweating. This would be her first real drop.

Jessica flipped through a book of printed checklists strapped to her thigh and read off the launch sequence.

Mahendra put a hand on her shoulder as he threaded by and pulled himself down into his seat. "*Magellan* is secure. We are ready for drop," he said.

"Roger that," Mac said. "Land ho."

A sliver of strange and wonderful light, real light, pierced the darkness of the hanger outside the cockpit windows.

"Hanger doors are open," Jessica said. "Umbilical detached, separation in five…four…three…two…docking clamps retracted."

The ship floated free for a moment, then Mac touched the overhead thrusters and they dropped slowly, silently, out of *Magellan*.

Space stretched out before them, overwhelmingly real, more black and more vast than any screen could render. The long, curved outer hull of *Magellan* arced overhead.

"The ship looks good," Evans said.

Off the port side they saw the planet, SL283a, a huge dark mass below them. They were coming up on another sunrise. Mahendra flipped down his star visor.

The dwarf star rose as they approached the terminus, that line that separated light from dark. Their landing site was down there in the grey area.

They dropped further and further away from *Magellan*.

Bands of dark clouds writhed at the edge of the night side, like spectral fingers reaching for the light. At the edge of the utter darkness, Mahendra could make out strange swirling formations, and movement that seemed somehow…unnatural. Looking at it made his stomach churn.

"Incredible," Blair said. "What is that?"

"It…it doesn't look like cloud formations," Chelsea said. She was breathing rapidly, just holding it together. Mahendra could hear the fear in her voice.

There it was, fear. He had it too. Mahendra had experienced it many times, but not like this. This wasn't fear of an engine malfunction, or a hull breach, or overheating in the atmosphere. This was something sinister creeping in from the edges of his consciousness.

"Whatever it is," Mac said, "we're about to get a lot better acquainted." He repositioned the ship so they were traveling backward and the swirling abyss of the planet's nightside was directly overhead. Then he hit the main engines to drop them out of orbit.

The force of the engines pressed Mahendra's back against his seat. They slowed rapidly and the gravity of the planet pulled them toward its center. The darkness of that swirling, writhing maelstrom of nightside chaos filled his vision. His pulse quickened and beads of sweat rolled back across his forehead.

When the engines cut out, Mac flipped the ship over. For a moment the nose pointed straight up, and all Mahendra saw were distant stars and the blackness of space. Then they leveled out, traveling forward again, with the underbody heat shielding angled for air braking in the planet's atmosphere.

It started with a shudder that shook Mahendra gently in his seat, a strange feeling, something you never felt in space. Quickly that shudder became a shake so violent that the straps of his harness pulled taught against him in every direction. The temperature in the cockpit steadily rose, and there was a sound like the roar of an engine only no engine had fired.

Jessica called out the altitude as they hurtled toward the surface of the planet, half gliding on the thin air. The shaking smoothed out, but the windows suddenly went black. Wind buffeted the ship, tossing them this way and that as they fell through the dark clouds.

"Bitch," Mac said, but he was totally focused on his job. The heads-up display fed him the information needed to make small adjustments to the ship's trajectory. They cleared the clouds and continued to fall. Then the VTOL engines fired, pressing them against the bottoms of their seats. The ship continued to drop toward the surface of the planet, the landscape still difficult to discern in the dim light.

The engines roared, but the rest of their increasingly slow descent tossed them about ever more gently. The landing struts deployed and Mac searched for a landing site until they were almost hovering over a patch of flat ground about 100 meters from the downed dropship. Their engines blasted everything around them as they touched down on the surface, kicking up so much debris that it was impossible to see anything at all. The ship groaned as it took on its own weight, then lurched suddenly as the engines cut out.

"What was that?" Mahendra said.

"We lost hydraulic pressure," Mac said, "on the left rear landing strut." But they were on solid ground, and he powered down the flight systems.

Jessica read off her checklists. Then they waited in silence for the dust to clear. When it finally did, they looked out over the blasted landscape of an alien world, a half dark realm.

Beyond the scorched soil and rock, Mahendra saw clumps of purplish black plants. And off on the far horizon, a dim red sun hung in the twilight haze, where he knew it would sit, unmoving, for as long as they remained there. He didn't feel the romance of adventure now. Perhaps it was because of the dropship out there, and the lost Langston Expedition, and the fear that grew in the shadowy edges of his mind.

MAHENDRA, BLAIR, and Evans stepped out of the dropship airlock and walked down the grated ramp to the surface. Chelsea's atmospheric analysis confirmed breathable air, and the temperature was a warm twenty four degrees Celsius. They wore full adaptive environmental suits as a standard precaution, and they were in touch with the onboard crew via radio comlink.

Jessica continued to attempt contact with any survivors of the downed ship, but they all felt that was just a formality now. If there were any survivors, they weren't listening.

Mahendra carried an electric ignition rifle with five rounds of stacked caseless ammunition.

He couldn't quite get used to the light here. Despite himself, he kept expecting it to change somehow, for the dawn to become morning, or for the dusk to become night, but it never did. A mist of water vapor blew through the landing site, but they could still see the glow of the red sun on the horizon. They walked around and inspected the ship.

"How's that landing strut look?" Mac said.

"Hydraulic shock is collapsed," Evans said. "There's some debris damage to the outer door. It may not close."

"She'll make orbit with gear down if necessary," Mahendra said.

"In theory," Evans said.

"We'll fix it when we get back," Mahendra said. "Let's go."

They headed off toward the other landing site. To their left, the grey world stretched out to an ominous horizon with tendrils of black cloud formations curling out of the distance like some hideous aurora. To the right, the far-off light of a searing desert burned in the distance.

The indigenous plants brushed against their legs as they walked. The plants were waist high, with broad black leathery leaves, all angled toward the red starred horizon. Some kind of purplish lichen grew on the exposed rocks, but there was no sign of any real animal life. The stillness of this world was only broken by the mist, and by a wind that gusted through the black leaves.

The gravity was less than Earth's, but it was still more than they were used to on *Magellan*, so hiking up the gentle rise seemed arduous at first. When they reached the top, they paused. On the other side of the rise should be the downed dropship, but they couldn't see it through the mist and dim light.

Mahendra led them on, following the beacon coordinates, down the gentle slope and across the plain. "It should be here," he said.

"I can hardly see anything in this mist," Blair said.

Then, out of the mist and the dark, they saw a hulk of metal, and the looming shape of a dropship above them. Evans arced the beam of a powerful hand-lamp across the hull. In the stark light the metal looked corroded, weather-worn, and covered in windblown dust. Mahendra figured it had been there a number of years at least. The ramp was down, its bottom edges buried in dirt. The airlock door gaped open, a darkness within.

"I don't know what we'll find in there," Mahendra said, "so be ready for anything." Mostly he wanted to be prepared for the seemingly inevitable discovery of the dead, men and women who had hurled themselves across the stars, just like they had, and never returned, people who had met their final, lonely end here in the depths of space, far from their families and any other semblance of humanity. Mahendra imagined his own wife and daughter waiting for his return.

They walked up the ramp and into the ready room, their helmet lamps and Evans's bright hand lamp illuminating the way. The metallic sounds of their footsteps echoed through the hollow interior of the ship.

There was no power on in the ship. The beacon must have been running off the backup power supply.

A coating of dust lay over everything in the ready room. Two environmental suits were missing from the racks, along with some survival gear. Other equipment looked like it had been discarded and lay scattered on the floor. Mahendra picked at a crumpled suit on one of the benches. It looked like somebody had been cut out of it in a hurry.

They proceeded up to the common room. The beams of their lights arced across the cramped, dark space. Again, dust covered the table and chairs, undisturbed. Used meal packets were scattered about the room, discarded and left where they lay.

Evans ran his hand across a wall. "What is this?" he said.

Dark stains mottled the grey plastic.

"Looks like blood," Blair said. There was a lot of it. Dried blood stained practically every surface in the room.

But there were no bodies. Mahendra deliberately slowed his breathing. "Let's check the bunks," he said.

The door was jammed, the plastic dented and the hinges bent. Mahendra pried it a little with his utility knife, then pulled it the rest of the way open.

The bunks were a disaster. Clothes, equipment, sleeping bags were strewn about. One of the bunks was broken, and there was more dried blood scattered across the room. There was no sign of anybody though, or any indication of recent activity. They searched the room for anything that might provide a clue to what happened, but found nothing.

They moved up to the cockpit. Mahendra and Evans climbed into the front seats, while Blair stood, his broad back bent beneath the low bulkhead.

Evans studied the various settings. He tried to switch on the main power but nothing happened. "The ship's been deliberately shut down, but it won't power up."

"Why is the beacon still running?" Blair said.

"The emergency beacon is connected to the power supply on an independent circuit," Mahendra said. "And there's a backup." Then to Evans, "Pull the log files and flight data. We'll analyse it later."

Evans popped open a panel, but where the ship's recorder should have been, there was just a gaping hole.

"All right, let's go," Mahendra said. "Back to the ship. We'll send up a drone to search for survivors."

Mahendra took one last look around the ready room as they left. It was impossible not to have expected something, and hoped for something else, but this confounded all their hopes and expectations.

"Captain!" Evans said. He and Blair stood frozen half way down

164 | A Darkquick Sky

the ramp.

Mahendra took a few steps to join them, then saw what they saw and stopped.

There was a break in the mist, and ten meters away a man stood still in the perpetual dusk. He was practically naked, wearing nothing but tattered rags about his waist. His eyes were shrouded in shadow. His long grey hair and beard blew in the wind. He stared at them. Then he raised a hand and waved.

THE MAN was a castaway, stranded on an alien planet for untold years. No doubt there were reasons for his behavior to seem off. But for many reasons, this was not how Mahendra had imagined any survivors. Mahendra expected the man to rejoice at his rescue, but if he did, he hardly showed it. He walked with a shifting gait, bare shoulders hunched, one eye squinting in the half-light. His first words were, "I didn't expect you."

Mahendra smiled behind the clear visor of his helmet. "We weren't expecting to find you," he said. "It was just plain luck."

"Luck," the man said, as if contemplating the meaning of the word. Then he cast a strange, searching gaze toward the dark side of the planet. His attention wandered.

Whatever had happened to his ship and the crew, Mahendra thought, no doubt his affect would be changed by years spent here with no hope of rescue.

"I'm Captain Mahendra Singh of the Planetary Explorers ship *Magellan*. What's your name?"

The man seemed to turn the question over in his mind, as if searching his memory for an answer. Finally he said, "Langston," as if he wasn't quite sure.

So this was Henry William Langston, Captain of the lost Langston Expedition. "Are there any more of you?" Mahendra said.

Langston stared at Mahendra, but said nothing.

"Captain Langston, are there any other survivors?"

Langston shook his head.

They returned to *Magellan*'s dropship with Langston. He went without question. Blair stooped to collect plant samples on the way. Evans gazed uneasily at the darkness on the horizon. Once inside the airlock, they waited silently as the decon cycle ran.

Mac wrapped a blanket around Langston as they came into the ready room, and Jessica handed him a pair of coveralls. Langston hesitated before putting on the clothes and looked uncomfortable in the cramped confines of the dropship. He kept looking overhead as if searching for the sky, only to shield his eyes from the bright lights.

An organic, but not an unpleasant odor surrounded Langston, something Mahendra could only identify as the smell of an alien world. Some measure of immediate hospitality seemed necessary, so the crew prepared a quick meal in the common room. It was strange to have a stranger among them.

Langston ate and drank hesitantly, and consumed little, muttering something about not being used to this food anymore.

After Langston had finished eating, Mahendra cleared his throat. "Captain Langston, how long have you been here?"

Langston stared at Mahendra and the crew. "I don't know." Then he laughed abruptly. "The world doesn't turn. I forgot about time a long time ago."

"How did you survive for so long?" Blair said. "Are the plants edible?"

"The plants," Langston said, as if it were a foreign word to him. He nodded. "Yes, they're edible. They have sustained me quite well."

"Forgive me for the questions I have to ask," Mahendra said. "But what happened? What happened to the dropship and the rest of the crew?"

Langston looked up toward the ceiling, but squinted and blinked at the lights. He shifted on the bench and scratched at his beard. "Madness," he said at last.

"Madness?" Mahendra said. Of course, people losing it in the depths of space was not unheard of. He had seen it on mining ships, but he had never heard of it happening on a Planetary Explorers expedition.

"Yes. My executive officer, Babo, went crazy. We had been out a long time you know. He sabotaged the ship and murdered three crew members in their sleep. He was in a violent rage. We had to shoot him. There were only two of us left, stranded here. Jackson committed suicide not long after." Langston nodded as if confirming his own story.

"Where are they?" Mahendra said. "Again, forgive me for asking."

"I buried them. Not far from my camp in the jungle."

"And the ship's recorder? Where is that?"

Langston hesitated. He should have known they would look for it, but he didn't seem prepared for the question.

"Do you remember?" Blair said.

"Yes, yes, I remember. I buried that too. I never expected anybody to come. Least not in my lifetime. And there were certain things, things Babo had done, that I didn't want record of."

Everyone was silent for a moment.

"It wasn't his fault, you see," Langston said. "It wasn't anybody's fault." He seemed about to say more and then stopped.

"What wasn't his fault?" Mahendra said.

"What happened!" Langston said, agitated.

"All right," Mahendra said, "and your starship, the *Armstrong*?"

Langston took a breath. "Gone. Orbital decay. Burned up in the atmosphere. Crashed into the light."

"What about those black clouds?" Chelsea said. "Do you know what they are?"

"No," Langston said, and looked up again, searching for a sky that wasn't there.

"That's probably enough for now," Blair said.

Mahendra nodded. "All right. We'll let you get some rest,

Captain Langston." But there was something about his story that didn't add up.

"I'll show you where you can bunk," Mac said.

Langston laughed. "Oh, I can't stay here. I have to go back, back to my camp."

"Captain Langston," Jessica said, "We're here to rescue you. We're going to take you home."

"You can't rescue me," Langston said. "This is my home now. I'm not going anywhere."

Jessica started to argue with him, but Mahendra held up a hand to stop her.

"All right, Captain Langston. I understand. But maybe you'll change your mind. Now that we've found you we're not leaving right away. Come again tomorrow, and we can talk more. Maybe you can show me your camp as well."

"Tomorrow," Langston said, as if the word had no meaning. Then he nodded. "You have many questions, Captain Singh. They will all be answered. Yes, they will all be answered."

MAHENDRA AND Jessica watched from the cockpit windows as Langston walked off toward the dark and disappeared in the murk and shadows. Mac and Evans had gone outside to patch up the landing gear. Blair and Chelsea were in the lab running a chemical analysis on some plant specimens.

"I keep expecting the morning to come," Jessica said.

"Or the night," Mahendra said.

"Anything."

"What do you think about Langston?"

"He's clearly been under a lot of stress."

"Do you think he's lost it?"

"I don't know," Jessica said "I mean…I can't imagine what he's been through…surviving here, thinking that nobody would ever come."

"But we did come, and we can't just leave him here," Mahendra said.

"Why not?"

"He's not in his right mind. It's our duty to bring him back."

"Maybe," Jessica said. She stared out the window. "I think those clouds are getting closer though. If we stick around we may find ourselves in one hell of a storm."

Mahendra put his hand on hers. "Don't worry," he said. "Mac will get us out of here, clouds or no clouds."

As if on cue, Mac's voice came over the radio. "Mahendra, are you there? Come in. We've got a problem out here."

"Mac, what is it?"

"I don't know. It's Evans. He fainted or something. His suit's working fine, but I can't wake him up."

Everyone sprang into action. They got Evans inside and onto a table in the ready room. Mac removed his helmet. His body was limp, his face unmoving.

Blair moved in and checked for vitals. Chelsea stood by with an external defibrillator.

Everyone stood silent, staring at Evans. Chelsea made a move, but Blair held up a finger. "Wait a minute. There's a pulse…and he's breathing, just barely. Let's get him out of this suit and to the lab."

They cut him out of the suit with a med-saw and carried him to the lab. The discarded suit caught Mahendra's attention for a moment. He remembered the suit they had seen on the abandoned dropship. They had cut somebody out of suit too. Did Langston's story account for that?

Evans was barely alive and completely non-responsive. Blair and Chelsea moved about the room, drawing blood, running tests, checking monitors.

"Well," Mahendra said. "What's wrong with him?"

"I don't know. I don't know," Blair said, shaking his head. "Maybe some kind of stroke. Maybe he came into contact with some kind of toxin, I don't know."

"Do what you can for him," Mahendra said. "And figure it out. We need to know if it's something environmental." He said to the others, "The rest of you prepare for a possible evac to *Magellan*."

Then Evans suddenly woke up. He inhaled deeply, blinked his eyes, and sat up, surprised to see all his shipmates standing around him. "Hey, what's going on? How did I get here?"

"You were outside working on the gear," Jessica said. "You passed out. Do you remember what happened?"

Evans tilted his head, trying to recall the last fifteen minutes of his life. "I remember being outside. Then…I remember…I saw those black clouds, like in a dream…swirling…moving. They reached out for me. They…spoke to me. It was in a language I'd never heard, but somehow I understood what it was saying."

"What was it saying?" Blair said.

"I don't remember."

"How do you feel?"

"I feel fine." He shrugged his shoulders at the stares he was getting. "Really. I feel fine. Just tired, that's all."

"You better get some rest," Mahendra said. "We're all exhausted. Jessica, you, Evans and Mac will take the first sleep shift."

MAHENDRA WENT outside to check on progress with the landing gear. He walked around the ship. He stared at the red sun on the horizon. Then he looked the other direction, toward the night, and the black clouds that stretched out toward him, shifting and writhing like the tentacles of some deep sea creature.

Jessica was right; the clouds were getting closer. Something about their twisted shapes made him sick to his stomach. Or maybe he just needed sleep. The perpetual twilight, the unmoving sun, was beginning to get to him. He had a feeling like time had stopped. And yet, if they didn't leave soon they'd be stuck, at least until the storm passed, if that's what it was. But he couldn't leave without Langston.

Mac and Evans had fixed the landing gear door, but the hydraulics were shot. They could be replaced back on *Magellan*, but not here. Maybe Mac could patch it. He was worried about Evans. Whatever had happened to him, Blair couldn't explain it. That made him nervous.

On his way back inside, Mahendra paused in the ready room. He removed his helmet and fixed it to one of the racks. Evans's discarded suit caught his attention again.

Mahendra checked Evans's helmet, seals, and life support unit. Everything looked in order. The suit itself looked fine as well, except where they had cut Evans out of it. He wondered again about the suit on Langston's ship.

Suddenly a low scream echoed through the interior, and shouting carried through the cramped space. Mahendra raced up to the main deck.

Chelsea was the first one there. She opened the bunkhouse door and a streak of blood spattered across her face. She screamed. Mahendra shouldered past her. Evans had gone berserk. Mac flailed against the bunks with a gaping neck wound spurting blood. Evans attacked him again, biting Mac like a rabid animal, his face red with blood.

Jessica was trying to pull Evans off. Mahendra joined her and together they yanked Evans back. The engineer turned and came at Mahendra in a violent frenzy, his eyes filled with blood lust, twin pools of chaos and darkness.

Mahendra stumbled back, arms up to defend himself, but Evans was on him in a fraction of a second. He bit one of Mahendra's arms and swept the other aside. Evans pressed Mahendra against the lockers, his bloody teeth bared and snapping at Mahendra's neck.

Then Evans let out a gasp of breath. His grip weakened. Jessica pulled a utility knife out of his back and stabbed again and again until Evans fell to the blood slick floor where Mac lay, collapsed in a heap, already dead.

* * *

THEY BAGGED the bodies and stowed them in the ready room. They worked in silence, cleaning up as much of the blood from the bunkhouse as they could. Then Mahendra and the remaining crew sat in the common room to discuss the situation.

"Blair," Mahendra said. "What happened in there? What happened to Evans?"

Blair sighed and shook his head. "I don't know."

"Something happened to him, when he passed out. He was fine before that."

"He seemed fine just afterward too," Blair said, trying to work out the problem in his mind. "Perhaps some kind of contagion, a toxin or a virus we overlooked."

"Check everything," Mahendra said. "Langston was in here. If it's some kind of contagion any one of us could be infected."

"That wasn't Evans," Jessica said. "You all knew Evans. That wasn't him. That was…that was…something else."

"He said something about a dream when he woke up," Blair said. "He said the black clouds spoke to him. Maybe he really had gone insane. Maybe this place, the abandoned ship, that damned sky—"

"Who's going to fly the ship now?" Chelsea said. She was practically in tears. "We have to get out of here. We have to get off this planet!"

Jessica put an arm around her. "Mahendra and I can both fly the ship."

"And we still have to deal with Langston," Mahendra said.

"Don't you see though?" Chelsea said. "It's this place. It drove him crazy. It's driving us all crazy."

"Damn it, this is not madness," Mahendra said. "Something strange is going on here, and Langston knows about it." Mahendra got up from the table.

"Where are you going?" Jessica said.

"I'm going to find his camp. I'm sending a drone up. Then I'm going out there to find out what really happened to the Langston Expedition."

Mahendra went to the bridge and launched a drone. Jessica followed. He programmed the drone for an infrared search pattern in the direction Langston had gone, off toward the dark and the jungle of black plants that loomed in the distance.

"You think Langston's lying?" Jessica said.

"His story doesn't add up. He's definitely hiding something and I'm going to find out what it is."

They waited, watching the monitor. It didn't take long for the drone to zero in on Langston's camp, about three miles into the night. They could see his heat signature moving about beneath the tall plants. He was alone.

"I'm going with you," Jessica said, but Mahendra stopped her.

"You need to stay here with the ship. If anything happens to me, take off, get the others back to *Magellan* and go home."

Jessica nodded with reluctance, but one of them had to stay with the ship, and she knew it. She met Mahendra's eyes for a moment, and they embraced. Then Mahendra headed down to the ready room.

He suited up, slung a rifle over his shoulder, and headed out the airlock door.

MAHENDRA WALKED toward the dark, the dim star at his back, through the low black plants dotting the otherwise desolate landscape. The topographical data from the drone guided him onward. He watched the sky as he walked, and the black darkness that reached out of the distant night.

Jessica checked in with him periodically by radio. "Mahendra, you there?"

"I'm here. I'm all right." He was exhausted though. He hadn't slept in forty, maybe forty eight hours. His body was confused, weak, and rebelled against the thought of another step, but he pressed on.

He reached a place where the plants grew much taller, the jungle Langston had spoken of. They weren't trees exactly, but huge plant stalks topped with giant leathery fan-like leaves. The entire forest had evolved in the unchanging light, leaves all angled in the same direction and the stalks getting taller the further one went.

Beneath the leaves of the jungle, shadows prevailed, and it seemed as if Mahendra had gone much further into the night. In the beams of his helmet lamp, he could see only a few meters ahead, through dense clumps of thick vegetation.

"Mahendra…are you there?" The signal was fading.

"I'm all right. I'm losing you though."

"How's tha—"

Static.

Mahendra thought he heard one or two more fragments of her voice, and then she was gone. He pressed on. It wasn't much farther to Langston's camp.

He came to a clearing where a stream of water flowed through the forest. Langston was there, his back turned as Mahendra entered the camp.

Langston knelt before an altar fashioned from a flat boulder, his arms stretched toward the black clouds of night. On the altar were five human skulls, weathered and scarred.

Rain began to fall, pattering off the leaves of the jungle.

Mahendra unshouldered the rifle and approached. Langston didn't move. Mahendra called out to him, "Langston."

Langston stood slowly and turned.

"Don't move," Mahendra said.

"Imagine a being," Langston said, "a consciousness so alien and complex, so powerful, that we must seem like no more than insects to it. Like microbes even."

"What are you talking about?"

"A god! A living god, here on this planet."

"I need to know what happened to your expedition. What

happened to your crew, Langston?" He could see their skulls on the altar, their eye sockets empty, their jawless mouths silent.

"It has come among you then? One of your crew has been chosen?"

"Something happened. And I have a feeling whatever it is happened on your ship too."

"Babo was the first. We managed to sedate him. We tied him up, but confinement drove him even madder. He tried to chew his own face off, Captain Singh. Can you imagine? We tried everything, but when you see the truth, when the god of night speaks to you, your mind is changed forever."

"What is it, Langston? An infection?"

"You're not listening. Jackson was next. It comes to you in a dream. If you're asleep you might not even remember. Then you belong to the god of night. You are his, and he dwells inside you."

"You're saying there's some sort of consciousness here, an alien that can control the human mind?"

"Then me." Langston smiled. "They couldn't stop me. I...I tore them to pieces...I ate their flesh."

"Who sabotaged your dropship?"

"I did. After the others were gone, I had a moment of doubt. I had to make sure I never left this place."

"You're insane."

Langston laughed. "What difference does it make?"

Lighting streaked across the sky, and the dark clouds billowed out of the night, stretching out across the twilight.

"It's coming," Langston said. "You should give yourself to it. You will feel so much better. I've come to terms with the things I did. You will too. It's a small price to pay for such an honor."

Langston took a step forward.

"Stay right where you are," Mahendra said.

"I do miss the taste of blood though...and flesh." Langston took another step.

"Stop!" Mahendra raised the rifle and aimed.

Langston charged, mouth open, teeth bared, screaming.

Mahendra pulled the trigger, and Langston fell in a heap to the ground, with a hole blown through his head.

JESS'S SIGNAL came in again near the edge of the Jungle. "Mahendra, are you there?" Her voice crackled out of the helmet speaker, half drowned out by the rain, but right away he could tell something else had happened.

"I'm here. What's wrong?"

"Mahendra! Mahendra, it's Blair." Her voice was stressed to the point of breaking, on the verge of panic. "He's gone crazy. It's too late. Oh, God, I'm so glad to hear your voice. I thought I was the only one left."

"Slow down. What happened?"

"I was up in the cockpit. I must have dozed off for a minute and something woke me, a noise, down in the lab where Blair and Chelsea were working. I went down to check it out. I opened the door. Blair had lost it, like Evans…only worse. He…Chelsea was…oh, God, Mahendra, I think she was still alive."

"Where are you?"

She seemed to have to think for a moment. "I'm in the cockpit. Blair came after me. I just ran. I'm so sorry, I just ran, I locked myself in here."

"Stay right where you are. Start prepping the ship for takeoff. And don't open that door until I get there."

"I can hear him out there."

"Don't move. I'm on my way."

Mahendra ran across the open landscape. He ran through the rain. A dark sky loomed above him, reaching for him like a writhing mass of black tentacles.

He ran all the way to the ship. Jess waved to him from the cockpit window. He raised a hand and signaled her to stay put. Then he unshouldered the rifle, walked up the ramp and went in the outer door. When the air exchange and decon finished, he removed his helmet and tossed it aside.

The inner door opened. Mahendra stepped into the ready room, looking down the barrel of the rifle. The ship was quiet.

"Blair?"

He scanned the shadowy corners of the empty room, waiting for a reply.

Silence.

The lab door was cracked open, the light on inside. Mahendra moved across the room, keeping a wary eye on the ladder leading up to the main deck. He nudged the lab door open with the rifle. Blood on the white walls. Blood everywhere. And what was left of Chelsea Fleet. Mahendra looked away and choked down an impulse to vomit.

He moved over to the ladder and aimed the rifle up through the opening to the main deck. Nothing.

Mahendra climbed the ladder with one hand, holding the rifle in the other, and stepped out into the cramped common room.

"Blair?"

The room was quiet. The faint metallic patter of rain on the hull echoed through the ship. Toward the back, the bunkhouse and the storage locker doors were closed.

Mahendra looked forward to where the cockpit bulkhead door was sealed shut.

When he turned back Blair was already upon him. He tried to bring the rifle around but it was too late. The knife in Blair's hand arced toward him.

Mahendra thrust the rifle out crosswise, barely blocking the blade.

The doctor had painted his face with blood. He pushed Mahendra back against the bulkhead, growling like an animal. He pushed against the rifle between them, trying to bury the knife in Mahendra's neck.

Mahendra started to sink down, pressed against the wall. Blair leaned in. Mahendra pulled the trigger and the gun went off, startling Blair for a fraction of a second. In that moment, Mahendra pushed the knife aside. Blair fell forward and Mahendra moved behind him, slipping the rifle over his head and choking him with it.

Blair coughed. His arms flailed and the knife clattered to the ground.

Mahendra pulled savagely. He felt Blair's trachea collapse beneath the rifle, and kept pulling, hard as he could. Blair struggled a little longer, then his body went limp. Mahendra kept pulling, even as Blair's body slid downward.

At some point the cockpit door had opened, because Jess was there.

"Mahendra, let go. It's okay. He's dead."

Mahendra let go of the rifle. Blair's body dropped to the floor and fell sideways. Mahendra took a breath.

"Where's Langston?" Jess said.

"Langston's dead. Listen, you said you fell asleep in the cockpit earlier. How long?"

Jess shook her head, confused.

"How long were you asleep?"

"I just dozed off. Just a few minutes. That's all."

Mahendra thought a moment.

"What?" Jessica said.

"Nothing. We need to get out of here."

THE SHIP was already prepped—they skipped the preflight checklist—and within minutes they took off, blasting upward through the rain. The sky above had gone completely dark, swirling with a menacing chaos of black clouds. Those roiling shapes somehow seemed to move with intent and purpose, with a mind of their own, although it was a mind beyond all human comprehension.

Mahendra shook in his chair, held fast by the harness, his hands wrapped around the controls. Jess was beside him, her head pressed back as they accelerated.

"That rear strut is still out," Jess shouted over the roar of the engines. "Landing gear won't retract."

Mahendra just nodded. The ship climbed higher, gaining speed.

They ascended into the dark maelstrom above. The windows went all black, and the ship shook violently, tossed about by the wind and madness. Mahendra tried to hold it steady, but they lurched and turned and shook until it seemed the ship would break apart, and they lost all sense of direction.

Mahendra thought for a moment they would die soon. Then the ship broke through the clouds into the clear upper atmosphere, and they rocketed into the vast emptiness of space.

The engines cut out, and Mahendra felt a surge of nausea as gravity released them. The ship was silent. Jess reached out and took his hand. They met each other's eyes for a moment and smiled with relief. The ship was on autopilot. They would rendezvous with *Magellan* in three hours. But there was still one more thing that had to be done.

Mahendra bagged up Chelsea's remains while Jess floated Blair's body down into the ready room. In the lab, Mahendra cleaned up as much blood as he could—not an easy task in zero gravity—and met Jess out by the airlock.

Jess was already in the airlock, lining up Mac and Evans and Blair as respectfully as possible along the outer door.

Mahendra floated Chelsea's body to her. Then he sealed the inner door, trapping Jess in the airlock.

Jess looked surprised, confused. She floated over to the window and looked out at Mahendra.

Mahendra pressed the intercom. "I'm sorry," he said. "I'm sorry, Jess. It's just for a little while."

He could see her thinking for a moment. Her hand went to her mouth when she realized why he had locked her in there. "You think I'm infected?" she said. Her voice sounded strangely disconnected, abstract, coming out of the speaker.

"I just had to be sure," he said. "You said you dozed off."

"What about you? How do I know you're not infected?"

Mahendra considered it. He didn't remember losing consciousness. But could he be sure he hadn't dozed off at some point? Could he really be sure? "We'll just have to wait and see," Mahendra said.

"But I'm the one in the airlock!"

"It's just for a little while," Mahendra said.

Her face went through a convulsion of expressions: anger, thought, resolve, impatience, then fear. She looked behind her, at the bodies of their crewmates lined up against the outer door. She looked back through the window. A look of fear came across her face such as Mahendra had never seen before, a look of sheer terror.

She almost struggled to speak. "Mahendra?"

"Yeah?"

"I don't want to live like that."

"I just had to be sure. Maybe now that we're off the planet—"

"Listen to me," Jess said. "If I go crazy like that, I want you to open the outer door. I don't blame you. I *want* you to do it."

"Jess...."

"Promise me," she said.

Mahendra nodded.

The change came quickly. Her face grew slack, her eyes blank. She looked around strangely, with some new and alien purpose. Then her hand shot out as if to reach through the window, but she only succeeded in pushing herself away from the door. She flailed backward, moaning and writhing in the empty air. She bumped into the bodies, pushed off Blair, and launched herself toward Mahendra.

Jess's face smashed against the window. She floated back again. Blood flowed from her nose and took flight, a trail of red droplets floating through the air. She pushed off the outer door and launched herself at Mahendra again, her face smashing against the window a second time.

Mahendra opened the safety latch for the outer airlock door. Then he put his hand over the button that would blow his shipmates out into space.

Jess hissed and growled, clawing at the blood smeared window.

Mahendra's hand trembled. "I'm sorry, Jess." He half choked on the words. He wept, unable to look away from Jess's distorted face. Her eyes no longer radiated the light he had known, or the warmth he had loved. There was only darkness now, a darkness that seemed at the heart of a dark universe.

"I'm sorry," he said. He pushed the button, and Jess tumbled backward as the door opened, her screams silenced forever by the unending void.

MAGELLAN'S VAST machinery surrounded Mahendra like a tomb, and he moved through her like a ghost, alone, and numb to the horror of his thoughts. The beige walls and the bright lights of the habitat seemed sterile and harsh, but for once he was glad the ship had no windows. He didn't want to see the planet below. He didn't want to look into that darkness—whatever it was—ever again. He set an outbound course, strapped in, and fired up the engines to break orbit.

Even when the ship was well on its way, he was afraid to sleep, and when he did his dreams were plagued by unspeakable nightmares. Nevertheless, as time passed it seemed likely he had escaped the fate of his crewmates. After a week he set a new course for Earth and engaged the hyperspace transfer.

Before bedding down for the long cryosleep—a thought which filled him with dread—he recorded his final log file:

I, Mahendra Singh, in the forty eighth year of life, resign my position with the Planetary Explorers. It is my intention to retire to my home in Rajastan, and to live out my days there. I only hope my wife and daughter can forgive me for the years I have been gone, and for the things I have done. And that some shred of peace will be left in my troubled mind.

Then he prepped for the long transit, stripped down, and got into his cryosleep bed. The lid closed, and the white walls of the bed surrounded him, like a cocoon, from which he could only hope to emerge to the dawn of a new day on Earth.

He was done searching. There were still wonders out there to be found, but he had found something horrible. His romance with the stars had ended, clouded over by a darkquick sky.

Matthew Lowes grew up with a deep love for fantasy and science fiction, and has since made writing his life's work. His stories have appeared in a variety of publications, including *Dark Recesses, Anotherealm,* and *The Lovecraft eZine.* He has traveled widely, from the deserts of Australia and West Africa, to the jungles and mountains of South America and Southeast Asia. Over the years he has been a pilot, a scuba diver, a rock climber, and a long time student and teacher of martial arts. He is currently working on a trilogy of fantasy novels, a collection of horror stories, and two roleplaying games. Lowes lives in the Pacific Northwest, where every day he pursues the dreams and ideas that are the inspiration for his work. Find out more at his website, matthewlowes.com.

Call to Action

Dear Reader,

Thank you for buying *ShadowSpinners: A Collection of Dark Tales.* I hope you enjoyed it.

As a small, independent publisher, ShadowSpinners Press doesn't have a marketing budget. If you enjoyed this volume, please help spread the word and support the creation of another collection of dark tales by writing an Amazon review, rating the book on Goodreads or telling a few friends about the book.

Thank you from all the contributors and worker bees here at ShadowSpinners Press.

Happy Reading,
Christina Lay

P.S. Keep in touch with ShadowSpinners via our blog, **shadowspinners.wordpress.com**.

74086451R00115

Made in the USA
San Bernardino, CA
12 April 2018